Y0-BCK-231

PRISONER BORN

BY CLAUDE AVELINE

Prisoner Born
The Fountain at Marlieux
Carriage 7, Seat 15
The Passenger on the U

PRISONER BORN

Claude Aveline

TRANSLATED FROM THE FRENCH
BY MERVYN SAVILL

Doubleday & Company, Inc., Garden City, New York
1971

To S. M.-C.

All of the characters in this book are fictitious, and any resemblance to actual persons, living or dead, is purely coincidental.

LIBRARY OF CONGRESS CATALOG CARD NUMBER 70–157622

PRINTED IN THE UNITED STATES OF AMERICA
FIRST EDITION IN THE UNITED STATES OF AMERICA

PRISONER BORN

WE ARE not friends, Philippe, and although we have known each other for twenty-three years, this is the first time I have called you by your Christian name. But the room I am now in, the plan I must carry out before I disappear, all that inspires me to write to you tonight and in the days to come—for unfortunately I shall not have finished in one night—makes you closer to me than a brother, my second half. Forgive me if these words offend you. We are at opposite ends of the social scale: you are a well-known and much-admired man who one day will be famous: I—well, everyone knows under what circumstances my portrait appeared on the front page of the newspapers! And yet there was your handshake yesterday and the look you gave me. And the loan. I had no need of it, for I have more than four thousand francs of my savings. But I *had* to ask you for it to test the forbearance of my only remaining sympathizer. One more thing—a memory.

We were eleven, you perhaps about twelve. I had gone out one Sunday with my father. He had a day off that Sunday, but had not changed his tunic or taken off the company's cap—a uniform which I found shameful. I loved him, Denis, but I could not stomach his livery on such a Sunday in that Avenue Henri-Martin full of new cars, private carriages, arrogant coachmen and all those rich people, laughing and wearing flowers. My father did not care in the least. Each time a tram passed he greeted the driver and the ticket-collector by name, calculated the excess passengers on the cars going towards the Bois and rejoiced for his colleagues' sake when he saw them return empty.

I walked along with my eyes glued to the ground and with a beating heart, throwing scared glances around me every few yards. I was terrified lest one of my comrades might appear, which would have been a catastrophe. And then, near the rue des Sablons, I caught sight of you. You were alone and beautifully dressed in a blue suit I had not seen before and a blue beret. You were walking towards us, and I thought I should die. Did you read nothing of this in my eyes? Your own lit up with a frank gleam like they did yesterday. Then, as we passed each other, you saw my father and took off your beret, just as in the school courtyard we used to greet the headmaster of the chief superintendent.

For twenty-two years I have wanted to thank you for that greeting. Oh, I know it was only the politeness of a well-brought-up child; but at that moment you gave me the only feeling of happiness in my life which has lasted until today. You made me realize that I was afraid of humiliation, not for myself alone but for my father, that I was not a bad son and many other things besides. From that day I gave you my affection. It has never been of the least use to you. I should never have known how to show it. It did, however, lead me towards you yesterday, and drove me to ask you for money I did not need. All that is impossible to express, Denis, and I find myself once more surrounded by walls; but you will understand.

You could have refused to receive me. Your kindness and charity are well known, but this time you had neither an unfortunate nor a poor man to deal with. I was a thief, a crook, who admitted his mistakes without affording the least explanation, and who that morning had been released from prison. During the few minutes I was waiting for you in your study among your books in a normal home, in the artificial silence of Paris, I asked myself—I must tell you everything—whether your interest as a writer had not prompted you to receive me. 'The Case of André Gallon', 'The Mystery of André Gallon', 'An Incredible Silence' . . . those ridiculous headlines in the newspapers!

As soon as you entered the room I was ashamed of my thought. You did not ask me a single question, either direct or implied, for it cannot be called a question to ask an old school friend how he is bearing up in his wretchedness, and how one can be of service to him. Until then the idea had not entered my head to borrow money from you: I did so under the pretext of starting a new life, and asked you for two or three hundred francs. You gave me five.

My debt to you is incalculable. Not the monetary debt, of course (I still have your banknotes and they will be returned in this letter), but for those few gestures which broke through my solitude. They will not alter anything and I shall not start a new life. I have been dead for seven years, and it is my corpse that speaks and walks while awaiting the hour of vengeance: once this is accomplished it will fall into decay. As there exists at least one being whom I esteem and admire, I owe him an apology. You shall have it.

Since yesterday I have been living in a hotel at B—— sur-Loire, a little town near Orléans. The man I am looking for lives here. From my window I overlook his house, which is on the far side of the street beyond a tiny garden. This is not a question of chance. Since the end of last year I knew that everything must go easily and simply.

This morning when the chambermaid came in with my breakfast (a chambermaid and a tray, Denis, after fourteen months in the Santé and six years at Melun—it was laughable!), and I asked her with every imaginable precaution where the house of this man was, and she replied to me that I could see it from my bed, I felt no surprise. It had to be thus. And even his absence—he will be returning in only a few days' time, at the beginning of next week—was ordained by fate so that I could acquit myself in your eyes. I know that when I have finished my story he will be there, and then that neither he nor I will be here any more.

After I had washed and dressed—and it was a real clean-up—I installed myself near the window to watch the house. My curtain, yellow, rather soiled and untransparent, prevents me from seeing clearly. On the other hand, it gives me all the protection of a wall. Once I stretched it out with my hands and pressed it against the window-pane; I shall not do that again, for no one must suspect my presence here. Obviously no one, not even he, could imagine it is I who am staying here, for I have registered in my mother's name, and my features have changed completely, as you yourself must have noticed. I have lost more than a stone in the past seven years; during the last few weeks I was allowed to let my moustache and beard grow.

When I left your house I bought a rather more presentable suit, a hat and an overcoat. At the same time as this writing-block and the revolver. No, nobody could possibly recognize me. But it is never a good thing to evince too much curiosity for fear of arousing it in others. My question to the chambermaid was quite sufficient. She is somewhat imprudent, and after all, I have seen quite enough through this curtain.

I know the look of the house by heart, and I can describe it to you, although it is now night and my shutters are drawn. A ground floor and upper storey in fine stone, with two windows on each side of the door and five on the first floor. Set in the slate roof, which is the same height as my window but seems lower because of the distance, are three round windows with cruciform panes. No balustrade. The drawing-room is on a level with the garden, which is hardly more than a little gravelled courtyard, bordered on each side with gay flower-beds, a mass of wallflowers and irises, box and daisies. Everything is very well kept, the box carefully trimmed and the gravel raked. The right-hand wall separates it from another house, with fronts on to the pavement; it is covered with ivy up to the roof. The gravel finishes with a crazy-pavement path leading from the front door to the garden railings. There is a wrought-iron gate with a letter-box. On the right pillar a bell with a chain, and beneath it a copper plaque which I have not been able to decipher from here but which must bear his name. The railings are set on a little low wall which curves to the left to rejoin the house, for on this side there is a narrow passage leading from our street to the Loire quay. The back must look out on to the river. A wistaria runs along the grille and only stops to allow the door to be opened. If it were not cut short there it would overrun everything. A prison of flowers, *mon cher*.

At this hour the men in Melun are asleep in their cells, exhausted after their day's work. How surprising it is to have an electric switch at one's disposal! Last night I used it a dozen times in succession. After the third time I had forgotten why, but continued automatically. In any case, for me there is no difference between night and day. Did you know that an obsession can haunt you for years, even when you are asleep? So much so that at first I thought when I woke up that I had not been asleep. I used to think that I should be able to relax on my first night of liberty; not on account of the bed–for I should be incapable of saying whether the bed in gaol was good or bad–but because it ought to denote the beginning of the end. But no, I dreamed just the same and woke up this morning in the same state as usual.

How peaceful and intimate it all is! . . . I am still thinking of the house. There appear to be a woman and children. After lunch I saw a young woman in half-mourning leave the house. If it is his wife she will not have to change her costume very much. I could not see her face very clearly, for as it was chilly she was wearing a large cape and a fur. She returned in the middle of the afternoon accompanied by two other ladies, one of whom was also dressed in black and the other in a light dress. The latter was laughing. During her absence the postman passed. He slipped the newspapers in the letter-box and rang the bell. Then, without waiting, he continued his rounds. After a moment a window was opened on the ground floor, but no one came out of the house. The bell echoed for a long time afterwards.

This street seems to be rather a busy one. I have heard footsteps, snatches of conversation and the noise of cars; but I could not see what was happening on the opposite pavement, and besides, the only thing that interests me is the house. Shortly before nightfall the woman in the light dress closed the shutters on the first floor and a plump woman with greying hair—presumably the maid—closed those on the ground floor. The house took on an air of abandonment. However, I remained behind my curtain, for I hoped to learn something more today.

It was quite dark when suddenly my door was opened. I got up abruptly. It was the chambermaid, who, thinking I was out, had come to turn down the bed. She apologized in a trembling voice, a little frightened by my presence there in the darkness. I explained to her that I had fallen asleep in my chair as I was very tired after my long journey. At this she began to laugh and went over to the window and closed the shutters. I could not prevent her, but turned my back while she was doing it and switched on the light at the last possible moment.

While she busied herself with the bed she remarked that to be as thin as I was I must have lived in hot countries, and yet she did not find me particularly sunburned. She said all this without looking at me, and I decided that she must have been watching me at other times, perhaps while I was having my lunch. I felt obliged to reply, unless I wished to arouse her curiosity further, so I invented a voyage to Africa. followed by an attack of malaria which had kept me in bed for several months. I soon saw that I did not interest her in the least and that she was not even proud of having guessed right. I think she was afraid of silence. In the dining-room she served my dinner without continuing the conversation. As soon as she had put my food in front of me she went over to the big table (I am the only one to have a small table to myself), where there were several cheerful men whom she obviously found more amusing.

I am back in my room once more. My second night at B——. How many more will there be? I have been writing to you for at least an hour, and my pen runs so fast that I have the impression of not even thinking, that it runs by itself. My breathing is very stertorous and I cannot understand why. Anyone would think there was a sick person in the room.

I must tell you everything.

YOU SAID in one of your novels—I cannot remember the exact words—that every man was marked for ever by his childhood. When I read that, just as I was beginning my adventure, just when I imagined that everything was going to change so marvellously, I revolted against such a statement. I remember I wanted to write to you. Had I done so you would not have seen me yesterday. I should have been too ashamed of my stupidity—I who know how right you were.

My life begins with my entrance to Janson, this life of mine which is going to end here. It has not changed. The little boy you knew with his black smock, the 'kid with the pinafore', whose satchel Palaiseau emptied one morning into the gutter in rue Scheffer, the one who in all the playtime breaks heard at least two or three of his comrades cry, "Ting-a-ling," or, "Tickets, please," and pretending to pull the tram cord. Yes, from the very first hour of the new term when the class burst out laughing at my black smock. I do not even know if you were there. You only began to exist for me after that Sunday when we met in the Avenue Henri-Martin. This proves that you were not one of the gang, for I knew them at once—Palaiseau, Ferrer, Bruneval, Cohen and The Twins. They sat all round me, and I immediately began to tremble.

These were my beginnings, and I dreamed of them nearly a year after the headmaster of my secondary school had advised my parents to let me try for a grant. My mother would not hear of this at any price. I to mix with boys of the upper class, which she hated; I, the son of a tram conductor and a charwoman! But my father insisted that this was just the chance to raise me above them and to make me become somebody. He spoke of the Rights of Man, and of his staff chief, whose father had been a simple ticket-collector like himself. I could not understand my mother's objections. In any case, at that time I did not know her as I grew to know her later. My parents' discussions hardly entered my thoughts, as I was thinking of something else—the *lycée*. I studied feverishly. I do not quite know when, or as a result of what, but Maman gave way, and I sat for my entrance around Easter. It was 1912 and I was not yet ten.

What a day! To start with, the exam was held in a *lycée*—I cannot remember which one; near the Panthéon, I think, but it does not matter. My father took me there before going to work and bought me two rolls for my lunch. At two o'clock I learned that I was eligible (I can still remember the dictation—*The Honour of the Dumonts*, by Edmond About), and later that I had been accepted. As my father had applied only for a non-boarder's grant, I obtained my studies completely free. I could enter Janson in the sixth form.

During my last month in secondary school I became estranged from my comrades. They did not wish to recognize that I was brighter than they were. Some of them even pretended their parents had said that without some pull I should never have got in and that some municipal councillor was at the back of it. Was this possible? Perhaps. But at that time I despised them for their jealousy and mediocrity. The boys at Janson well and truly avenged them.

During the summer holidays I went nearly every day to the Avenue Henri-Martin. Passing by the rue Decamps, the rue de Longchamp and the rue de la Pompe, I haunted the enormous building and studied every window. On my return home, in order 'to get on', I spent hours reading the books that M. Gabarel, my teacher from the rue Chernovitz, had lent me. My mother, who in her off time from charring made jumpers for a hosiery in the rue de Passy, pretended not to notice. She did not love me. I was born too late to take the place of a brother who had died, in his ninth year, of pneumonia, and she found me inferior to him in every respect. My father sometimes stuck up for me. He insisted, for example, that Henri had never given them the same satisfaction in his studies as I had. Maman scoffed at him. She maintained that studies had no connection with intelligence and particularly not with character. She treated me continually as a hypocrite and a coward. I could not understand what she wanted of me.

When I returned from Janson with bloody knees or merely with red eyes she jeered, and said that I had obviously not stuck up for myself. And it was true. From the day of the smock incident I had looked upon myself as an inferior being. I was the only scholarship boy in the class, and as my parents paid no fees I deserved no consideration. When they beat me I dared not even parry the blows. One day I cried out for mercy. Yes, for mercy, if you please. I remember the winks that Bruneval and Palaiseau exchanged, and the subsequent joy in their laughter. And I found everything quite normal—everything except my mother's contempt. The games master never noticed my plaints. In any case, I repeat, they were not plaints but appeals for mercy, and I never cried until I was on my way home from school. When they saw Ferrer, The Twins and others playing at tramways, they could not have understood the allusions, as they had no idea whose son I was. Like all the other pupils I had given my details to M. Florigny in class the first day. Only he could have understood their malice; but he never took recreation, and even then would he have intervened? When he singled me out in class and I stood up to reply, he never questioned me before having looked me up and down with an expression of disgust that made me lower my eyes with shame. The others always jeered at that moment, and he never dreamed of punishing them.

Two or three weeks after the opening of term he told me that they sold an article in the shops known as a comb, which was within the reach of the most modest purse. This was one morning when my father, after having done his hair, inadvertently stuck our comb in his pocket and went off with it. I do not know why, but I repeated M. Florigny's words to my mother. She took from a drawer, an old pair of shears, which I had never seen before and close-cropped my head. The following morning M. Florigny declared in class, "Well, well, your family certainly does not believe in half measures." They ceased there and then to call me the 'kid with the pinafore' and started to treat me as 'convict' and 'criminal'. Palaiseau related that I had escaped from Guiana and had derailed my father's tram. That was the day Bruneval spat in my face, saying that one could not treat convicts any other way.

All these memories come back to me this evening along with a thousand others, and I am telling them to you because they are important. But you see, Denis, those boys who tortured me mercilessly up to the time of my adventure now almost make me laugh. Everyone deserves what he gets. I was a dirty little coward and a traitor to our poverty. I ought to have spat in Bruneval's face and been prepared to be expelled from the *lycée*, for he would certainly have reported me. Then, as I was not strong enough to fight, I ought to have screamed in the courtyard and drawn the attention of all the 'beaks'. I ought to have let my hair grow and come to school with lice, and wiped my backside with my comrades' notebooks. If I hate my mother today it is not because of her unkindness–she was *right*–but because she brought me into the world as I am, or valued as I was. For I am no longer like that, and I shall prove it.

Then suddenly I saw you some time before we actually met. You were walking with Fournier in the playground, and you were both wearing mufflers. The results of the first French composition had just been announced, so it must have been towards the end of October. The two of you had tied for first place and I was third. Fournier looked at me through his spectacles, for I was alone in a corner, and I heard him ask you, "What's his father?" And you replied, "I don't know."

I remember it very well now, and I said to myself, Did they miss the opening class at the beginning of term, or have they really forgotten? One cannot forget such a thing. Yes, and when I met you later in the Avenue Henri-Martin the reason I was so frightened was that I thought: now he'll know.

Both you and Fournier certainly knew; but you, the two leaders of the class, could not be bothered with such trifles. For you it was no more than a trifle. Actually it would have been better had you attached some importance to it like the others, because you, as opposed to them, would have supported me instead of ignoring me. Oh, please do not think I am reproaching you. That would be the last thing . . . Besides, at that moment the others were already beginning to calm down. Everyone avoided me, but I was not attacked any more as I was during those first days. Perhaps this had something to do with Fournier and yourself, for you had got into the habit of shaking me by the hand, and that gang of ruffians respected both of you. I became a sort of zero, a cipher to whom the professors grudgingly gave good marks in spite of themselves. I was always in the first ten without ever being able to beat you. I told myself, however, that I was just as good as you but that I had to take a back seat because of my black smock and my scholarship. What conceit, don't you think, when we now compare the status of Philippe Denis, Louis Fournier and my own?

I must try to bring a little order into my memories. The more I jot them down the more they rise up in front of me. I have an idea that they are all demanding to be heard. My real trial begins tonight. I do not understand. I have no other thought but to avenge myself and die. I no longer exist and everything is a matter of indifference and . . . why write? To explain to you. That is why. You must forgive my incoherence. It seems that as I write I am unleashing terrible forces that have nothing to do with the past nor with what is going to happen—real monsters. So far I thought only of one thing and could only distinguish one image. Now I find this thing and this image suddenly encompassed by an infernal saraband or by motionless figures even more terrifying.

No, my childhood does not make me feel inclined to laugh. I can see my mother knitting next to the lamp which lit up only her hands and the table. Whenever I tried to draw near with my exercise-book or with what I was reading, she would say drily, without even looking at me, "Get away from there." I had to return to the shadow where my eyes watered from weariness trying to decipher my lessons. One day I had the courage to answer back. "The lamp won't use up the oil any quicker." This time Maman looked up and said, "In front of them you are like a dog and you dare to answer *me* back!" Then she blew out the lamp and continued to knit in the dark. I could hear the click of her needles. I remained there stupefied, without moving, until the moment came for her to prepare the dinner. She did not relight the lamp until then.

Is she still alive?

During the trial, Maître Gaillard, the young lawyer who

was in charge of my defence, went to see her. She was living in a little room in Belleville and was still a charwoman. He asked her to come and give evidence at the trial, but she replied that she had already been subpœnaed by the magistrate and that one journey was enough; that I had ceased to exist for her for a long time; that she understood nothing about my affair, but was not surprised that manipulators of money one day became crooks, after which she showed the lawyer the door.

She never or hardly ever beat me—far less than my father did, anyway—nor did she let me go hungry. The bed coverlet was always carefully darned, also my clothes. She kissed me on the forehead morning and evening, and I never returned her kiss—if one could call the contact of those pursed lips a kiss. . . . While I was going to secondary school she spoke to me several times a day, allowed me to play with my comrades on Thursdays and Sundays, and there was a certain gentleness in her behaviour. But once I went to Janson, after the disputes with my father on the subject of the scholarship, everything was finished.

Seven years ago she lived at 32 rue Clavel. Perhaps you would like to pay her a visit one day. She would not know who you were, for she has never read anything in her life; but you would know how to talk to her. You will be able to tell her how I died. She will not love me any the better, but all the same . . . After all . . . No, better leave her in peace. What good would it do? Anyhow, I hope she is dead—she too.

I remember that December evening when she came home about nine o'clock. My father had already been home some time from the depot and was worried because she was late. I had installed myself under the lamp, happy to have this unexpected opportunity. The room in the rue de l'Annonciation, where we all three lived and where I was born, a fair-sized attic room with a kind of recess for the kitchen, looked out on a backyard and on to a roof.

Every evening my mother covered the window with a thick, red-flowered curtain which she hung on two hooks. That evening no one had bothered about the curtain, and despite the reflection of the lamp in the window-pane we could see the opposite roof white with snow. My father was standing in front of the dying stove, which was only lit when absolutely necessary. It was very cold and we could hear the Puigs talking in the room next door. At last we heard a step slowly climbing the stairs. Maman usually climbed up quickly; but it was she right enough, with snow in her hair and in the meshes of her shawl. She went over to a chair and sat down at once—she who never sat down except when she was doing her knitting!

My father asked where she had been, and she replied, "For a walk." At this he began to swear at her, banging on his chest with his fist. She was haggard-eyed and paid no attention to him. Suddenly she saw me. She stood up and came over to me and lifted up my chin: I thought she was going to strangle me. My father fell silent, or rather he said to her, "What's he done now?" Then she began to speak very, very fast—as fast as I am writing to you this evening. She told me how she had been dismissed from her most important place, where she worked every day from two to six.

Do you remember de Bimont? That rather dumb boy who was always bottom of the sixth form? My mother, without knowing it any more than I did, for I had never heard her mention the name, had been employed by his parents. She spoke occasionally to my father about her daily work, but only mentioned her employers by their addresses. She would say, for example, "I'm going back to the rue de la Pompe today," or, "They've got whooping cough at the rue Raynouard." The de Bimonts were 'the Avenue Raphael'—the most opulent house, with a cook, chambermaid, butler, a chauffeur for monsieur and a coachman for madame, and where they hired one or two polishers for the parquet floors and a charwoman solely to clean the copper pans and the silver for their receptions.

Maman had seen Madame de Bimont that day. The lady had deigned to descend into the servants' quarters to tell her that she could not keep a person in her employment whose son went to high school and was in the same class as her own son. How had she found this out? Anyhow, Maman had been discharged on this account. Madame de Bimont had said she could not understand how anyone dared to have such ambitions when they were so poor, and that people should know how to keep their place. My mother was holding the bottle of liquid which she used to polish the pots and pans. She had thrown the contents over Madame de Bimont and ruined a *peignoir* worth 800 francs—more than my father earned in three months. The lady, in a fury, had threatened her with the police, and even tried to make her sign a paper promising to pay for the damage. Maman replied that she would rather go to prison, whereupon the butler threw her out into the street. Afterwards she had wandered about in the Bois not knowing where she was.

After almost every phrase she repeated, "All because of you, all because of you!" My father asked her why she had lost her head when she was usually so self-controlled. She replied that she would have liked to wreck the whole place and to have killed me into the bargain for courting the company of such people.

"We have to thank them for our livelihood," said my father with lowered head.

Maman looked at him with horror, and then burst out laughing. You cannot imagine what that laugh was like,

Denis. The neighbours stopped talking. Papa went over to her with clenched fists. I had never seen him raise a hand to her, but now he took her by the shoulders and shook her until she went limp before my eyes. Her laughter began to wilt, and she started to cry at the same time, "Naturally, naturally!"

I do not know what happened then, but I have the impression that I received a blow in the face. Was it a real blow or did I simply faint? When I regained consciousness I found myself on my bed. Maman was preparing the dinner and my father was sitting on a chair staring at me.

Like him, I thought that we had to thank the rich for our livelihood and that my mother must be mad. I was only frightened of one thing: de Bimont would be certain on the following day to tell the whole class. The next morning he actually did look at me in a strange manner, but did not open his mouth, and the class never heard about it.

I have suddenly begun to wonder whether somebody is spying on me, for I have just heard a noise in the next room like a hand sliding along the wall. There is no communicating door, but perhaps through a hole pierced in the partition. . . . Despite my efforts, I may have aroused someone's curiosity–the hotel keeper's, or even the police. It must be an hallucination. But one thing is certain: I am not living here like everybody else. I spent the whole day in my room until the maid surprised me in the darkness, and since dinner-time I have been writing. For how many hours? I have not had a watch for seven years. I forgot mine on the night-table on the day of my arrest, and it was sold with the rest of my belongings. I could, of course, have bought another one yesterday, but for so little time . . . ?

It cannot be far off midnight. I must have been writing for three hours. The noise of my pen for three hours, and particularly my breathing; they are entitled to ask questions about me. Or perhaps they have noticed the light between the slats of the blind. But after all, a *free* man has a right to keep his light on all night, to write for hours on end and to suffocate if he feels so inclined.

I never bothered to find out if you remain under observation by the police once you have finished your sentence. Do they go on considering you a dangerous individual . . . for some time, at least? Have I been followed since yesterday morning? I am trying to remember. Between Melun and Paris, at the Gare de Lyon, in front of your door, in the shops . . . *Mon Dieu*, suppose I was seen buying a revolver! However, I never noticed anything suspicious. How ridiculous! How could I be sure now as I never thought about it? I know nothing about sleuthing. If some good man followed me he must have been delighted to find so ingenuous a prey. Was it he who instructed the maid to ask me questions and to enter my room suddenly without knocking? Her pretext was a bit flimsy. . . .

Denis, if anyone tries to prevent me from carrying out my plan it will be so much the worse for him. It is impossible for anyone to come between the man I am looking for and me. I don't want to find myself in prison again. I want to die after having settled my accounts. Is that clear?

(*The following day: Saturday*.)

I DO NOT know what happened. I suppose I must have imagined that noise. It was repeated twice. I told you . . . like a hand sliding along the wall. I think I must have stopped writing and switched off the light. The darkness increased my fear. In seven years I have grown unaccustomed to complete darkness, so I tried not to move or even to breathe. After a long while I got undressed in the dark and went and bolted the door, a simple but practical little bolt that cannot be opened from the outside. I hid my revolver and these pages under my bolster. Then I lay down and waited. I believe I even slept at times; but I saw the dawn creep in through the shutters, heard the sounds of an alarm clock and people moving about. I unbolted the door so that the maid would not find it locked. She brought in my breakfast as she did yesterday, and her behaviour seemed quite natural.

Once dressed, I risked a gesture which might have cost me dear. On my return from the bathroom I purposely mistook my door and opened No. 15, from which I thought I had heard the noise. It was empty. The bed had not been turned down and the room resembled any normal hotel bedroom. I even noticed dust on the bedside table. At that second I thought how stupid it would be if anyone saw me leaving. For my plan! But I was lucky.

Luck . . . To write this word, Denis: luck. As the word exists, the thing must exist too, I suppose. You see, I had it too—and not only on leaving No. 15. Or at least I thought I had. What I really mean is: is there such a thing as luck? Or does one merely imagine it exists? There are words for things which do not really exist: happiness, for example, real happiness. Or real luck. And yet, the fact that I find myself here opposite his house, is that luck? That the only fellow prisoner in Melun with whom I could talk freely—I, who never uttered a word to anyone for ten years—happened to come from Orléans and knew him, is that luck? No, it is something far more serious. Luck is hazard which turns out well, whereas this was destiny, fate.

What a philosopher you are going to lose, don't you think? My pen certainly continues to write by itself. When I returned to my room this morning my only thought was to tell you what happened during the night and to continue with my confidences, but I had to go out so as not to repeat my programme of yesterday.

So I went out. The hotel proprietor treated me with great respect. He was sitting in the café on the left of the lounge opposite the dining-room and left his counter as soon as he saw me through the glass door. He had learned from the chambermaid of my fictitious journey to Africa and of my illness. He remarked that I still looked far from well. Then he asked me if I knew the neighbourhood and if I often came to these parts. Obviously my presence is difficult to explain in a place like this. The hotel caters only for commercial travellers, and a few local farmers on market days who prefer to arrive the previous evening. But in the summer, he told me, tourists like to stay here because of the church and the old houses in the main street, and he added with pride, "And also because of our specialities." His wife joined us and assured me that no one in the region knew how to cook a *matelote de Loire* or a *poulet sauté* like she did. They exchanged looks like a young married couple. Both of them seem to be very nice people. They presented me to their child, a little boy of four or five, fair-haired like themselves, who was laughing to himself and riding round the courtyard on his tricycle. Happy people, Denis, who show their happiness. They have no idea of the publicity I shall be bringing them.

I explained my presence by making use of what I had just learned. I mentioned that I was very keen on historic towns and that to write a description of my journey I had sought out a pretty background like B——, particularly as their hotel had been recommended to me. They were delighted.

I, who thought at Melun that I should never have any more need to tell lies, that my last days would be spotless. I lied to you about money, lied to the shopkeeper about the revolver and lied to the chambermaid and the hotel proprietors. It had to be. I must protect what I hold in my hands—two deaths. That of the man who destroyed my life, and my own. I can understand spies, Jesuits and renegades. Do you understand what I am telling you? The nearer I am to my goal the greater I feel. That grandeur of which I so often dreamed and which I sought in the mud.

I ought to have killed myself when I was small. There is something beautiful about an infant suicide—a soul that can bear neither injustice nor corruption, a kind of angel. My mother would have wept for me and would perhaps have considered me a hero. A child who kills himself because the sons of the rich insult and torture him. I never dreamed of it. On the contrary, I wanted to live, and at all costs, provided I could resemble those who really live, those whom we have to thank for our livelihood. I did not know how to. . . .

I did not know, or I never learnt the trick. Ah, now I am becoming arrogant again. No, I did not know how to, and now I dare to feel myself greater because I am going to avenge myself, because I am going to obliterate a loathsome and intolerable image. I am ashamed.

I have just plunged my head in a basin of cold water. What was I saying? I do not want to reread what I have written—not a line of it. So much the worse if I repeat myself or miss anything out. What is written is written just as what is done is done. To look back upon words when it is impossible to reverse actions? No, never on your life. One can perhaps efface but one can suppress nothing. There will be blood on the stone path which I looked at again just now, blood where he will fall. Good. The plump woman with the grey hair will come out, perhaps, with a large basin and a sponge and rub the stain until it is invisible. But he will have fallen there all the same. There will have been what they call a crime, just as there will be a suicide here with brains spattered on the carpet and the walls, and it will last as long as everything I have ever done and endured —for eternity. So what does it matter, I ask you, what does it matter?

That cold water was of no avail. My mind still wanders and my hand is trembling. That is wrong, particularly my hand. . . . I must be calm. What was I saying? Oh yes, that I had spoken to the hotel proprietors. Then I announced that I would go as far as the church before lunch. From the threshold the colours of the house leaped to my eyes. I was so hypnotized yesterday behind my yellow curtain and this morning it was so fine that I thought something had changed, that flags had been put out for a holiday. The shutters were open once more (I saw them being opened while I was washing), blue-grey shutters against grey stone. And the wallflowers, the irises, the daisies, the white gravel, the ivy and the box all gleamed in the sunlight and gave the impression of great joy. My heart beat faster, I assure you, but I passed by quickly, and if anybody had been watching they would have been unaware of my emotion. Now when I look up everything is yellow again because of the curtain.

Three children are now playing in the garden, the hotel keeper's fair-haired little son and two others, *his*. They may be five and two. The smallest is sitting on the ground scraping the gravel with a rake. The two larger children are chasing each other, and I can hear their shouts of laughter even through my closed windows. They were there when I went up to my room after lunch. No one has joined them. I suppose their mother must be in the study or the drawing-room. She may even have a boudoir and be writing to her husband. She must be telling him that all is well, that the children ask after their father every evening and that she is looking forward to his return. She is working on my behalf. I am in a hurry too. But at the same time since my walk I have felt a sort of pleasure in waiting, in saying to myself that I am here watching like a spider and that I shall catch the large fly when it approaches my web!

Enough of that. I will not raise my eyes any more. It is the past that I owe you, and the hours slip by.

Do you remember enough about me to recall the few successes I had at Janson—after you and Fournier? The last term in the Sixth Form second prize in French and second in mathematics (you had only a mention in maths and Nanot won the first prize) and 'adequate' in Latin and history. In the Fifth Form I obtained only an 'adequate' in French but second prize for mathematics and this time one for history. How I worked! My second year was a little easier than the first. I was hardly ragged at all, and a few of the boys even shook my hand on their return from the holidays. M. Tixier was not so harsh as M. Florigny and did not try to humiliate me. One day when he was at the blackboard and Ferrer wiped his feet on my cape, which was hanging near him, he noticed the fact and sent him out of the room. If we had had a professor in the Sixth like him, everything might have been different, but I never lost the feeling of terror which pursued me until my graduation. Admittedly, they left me more in peace, and I changed my seat to escape from that band of hooligans, but it was enough for me to catch their eyes across the classroom for me to begin to tremble. And then nothing had changed at home. Maman ignored me more and more, and now attacked my father at every opportunity.

In the middle of January a strike in the Company caused appalling arguments. My father did not approve of the trade union's decision and thought that they should have waited.

At this, my mother treated him as a beggar, a money-grabber, because on his route–Avenue Henri-Martin-Gare de Lyon–the regular passengers, rich people, often gave him a small tip. She had just taken her bus one day and saw him touch his cap in thanks to a passenger, and she, who never wept, wept the whole evening. Twice she put on her shawl to leave us, on evenings as cold as the one on which Madame de Bimont had discharged her, and I flung myself at her feet, imploring her not to go. Once she even went down the stairs, but my father ran after her and had to promise that he would support the strike. This did not prevent him from treating her as a mad woman. He told her that she would have gained a lot when we all starved to death. "So much the better if we do die," she replied, "if it makes others understand and makes them rebel."

"All the same," my father replied, "you go to work with the rich."

I can still see her at that moment. They had just come up the stairs again and she had not yet taken off her shawl. I was shivering with fright because I said to myself that if we made her angry again she would leave and never come back. It is difficult to explain why I wanted her to stay when I really detested her! She gave that little dry laugh of hers and reminded my father that she sent nearly everything she earned to the Party, and that was not going to give up doing so now. My father did not say another word. The more I think of it, the more I wonder by what miracle I was allowed to enter high school to carry on with my studies. Probably out of contempt. . . .

We were hungry that winter, even after the strike finished, because my father was grounded for a month. And I saw my mother really happy. She ate hardly anything and placed everything she could scrape together in the kitchen before my father with the words, "Come, eat it up." Nothing for her or myself. My father then offered us each a portion from his plate, but she refused hers. She nibbled a chunk of bread and said to me, "You ought to be ashamed of yourself, depriving your father of food—he needs his strength!" They still quarrelled. And then, one day, we began to eat as before.

It was in the spring of that year—as we parted company in the Fourth Form—that you invited me one Thursday to come and play at your house. Fournier, Nanot, Muzillac and all the best fellows were to be there. In what a state I arrived home! I thought that Maman would understand at last . . . Understand? How could she possibly know who you were? And even if she had, she would only have contrived to make it recoil upon me. It was better to mention the invitation casually. How my voice trembled! I did not say very much, only, "Denis has asked me to play on Thursday." To play at Denis's, I kept repeating to myself. I had no idea what we were going to play at your house, because I had only played with street children.

Is the apartment you live in today by any chance the same one as your parents had then? No, that's impossible, it is too far from Janson and you would have gone to another school. And yet I cannot help thinking at this moment . . . I can see us playing in your study, in the room where the day before yesterday you gave me those 500-franc notes with such a look of sadness. . . .

I had waited the whole evening until it was time for me to go to bed. Maman was washing up: my father was on duty and we had had supper alone in silence. I remember I went over to her and made my remark. She wiped her hands and took my trousers off the back of the chair where I put my clothes; it was the only pair I possessed, for as a result of the strike we had been living on our savings, and as my spare ones had worn out during the winter I was wearing my Sunday pair every day. I was hard on my clothes and it was now not much better than the others had been. My mother had put a patch in the seat—of the same material, but the colour was much newer. I assure you it was hardly noticeable, but Maman held it up to the light, and the patch stood out like a huge circle. It was hideous. She merely said, "Have you said you'd go?"

I told you on the following day that I could not come. You replied, "Well, it will have to be some other time." Some other time! Yes, yesterday. Of all the bitter memories of my youth this haunted me the longest. You see, the shears and the lamp seemed merely to be my mother's malice, whereas the patch in my trousers was poverty and misery.

Today I realize that Maman was always trying to make me rebel against the conditions of which we were victims, we and all the others who were being exploited. She achieved the opposite effect. I kept telling myself that I must earn money to buy fine clothes, to go to the theatre or on holidays, and above all to go and play with you. Later, when I thought of my own children, I said that I must bring them up like rich children—like those I can see in the garden now, *his* children. They are well dressed, you know. The baby has on a bathing-costume which leaves his chubby little back bare. The other is wearing shorts and a sleeveless shirt. In the old days I often dreamed of such children, and of a woman I should love who would take them on her knees, who would spoil them, like a real mother. And I, with my heart full . . .

Nothing ever turns out as one expects. He, for example, with his nature, with his incredible luck—well, he will never see his children grow up. At least I pray that he will not die instantly, but have the time to realize what has happened.

I have not much to tell you about the Fifth. The distribution of prizes took place on the 12th of July at the Trocadéro and on the 6th of August my father went off to war. Not far away at the start. He was already forty-four and on the territorial reserve, and he was sent to guard a bridge near Villeneuve-Sàint-Georges. When I look back on those days, one name rings in my ears: Jaurès. For Maman and for my father, too, the war, and all the evils of the world, resulted from that assassination. Now Jaurès was dead anything could happen. Father related the tragedy as if he had been present: Jaurès sitting on a café bench surrounded by his friends and the assassin hidden behind the window. . . .

What a parallel, Denis: this story which I listened to with such terror at twelve, and now myself behind a window with a weapon in my pocket. I wish I could remember more details about the assassin. The first point: was he in practice? Isn't a man who has never used a revolver bound to miss his target the first time? The armourer assured me that with a Browning like the one he sold me, which had both a rear sight and a fore sight, I should be able to hit my adversary at twenty-five yards with no possibility of missing. (I told him that I lived in the country and that every night a thief came and stole my chickens.) He even added: "With a calibre of that size" (.303 it appears; I have had to pierce a hole in my pocket because the barrel is so long) "nobody would dare to come nearer than that or he would be a dead man. Anyhow, you know yourself."

"Of course," I replied. It was not true. I fired a rifle in the regiment, but I have fired only a revolver at fairs. You can take your time and the target is stationary. One day, when I shot at a ball moving on a jet of water, I amused the onlookers and had to laugh myself: I broke four pipes at the back of the booth, and the ball still went on jumping about in front of my eyes. No, I do not know how to, but I shall know, because I *must*. I have eight bullets at my disposal, seven of them for him, and some power will guide my hand. Otherwise there would be no justice—and that, there certainly is.

Only after my father had gone away did I realize the

place he occupied in the house. Our room suddenly appeared so vast and dead. He was rather a big man with a loud voice, and when he laughed Maman used to say, "Ssh, you'll wake the neighbours." When he sat down he always stretched out his legs and unbuttoned his tunic and the top button of his trousers. Now he was no longer there I thought of him constantly, and would have loved to jump on his knee and tug his moustache—which, of course, I had not done for years.

In the Avenue Henri-Martin I watched *his* car pass—a brand-new tram, for the line had been electrified at the beginning of July. A woman had taken his place on the platform, but his friend Ferrand still drove: I could not quite understand why, as Ferrand was younger than my father and should have gone to the front like the others. Maman said "Good morning" and "Good night" and that was all. She knitted more than before, as nearly all her employers had fled from Paris. I wandered about the empty streets or she would send me to wait in the grocer's queue for a little coffee or sugar. She had begun to drink a lot of coffee, perhaps as a substitute for food, which had become scarce. Decidedly a bad year for the stomach!

Do not ask me what I thought about the war: I should have liked to be a soldier, to have killed Huns, and I was grieved to know that my father was far behind the lines. Vinet, our porter, was wounded at Charleroi: I felt proud of him and ashamed of us. I remained for hours in front of the newspaper kiosks in the Place de Passy reading the *communiqués* and looking at the photos in *Excelsior* or on the front page of the *Petit Journal Illustré*. On my return home I sometimes tried to start a conversation. I would say, for instance, "We seem to have won a battle."

"Well, what of it?" my mother would reply, without looking up from her knitting.

A little later she acquired the habit of talking to herself at table. The first time I thought she wanted to talk to me and I replied, but by the way she suddenly raised her head I could see that she had forgotten my very existence and that I counted for her no more than before. So I continued to keep silent, and after a few days did not even listen to what she was saying. Today I ask myself whether this was not an indirect way of addressing me all the same. My father's absence weighed upon her too, and perhaps at that moment I could have grown nearer to her. I think I must have disappointed her terribly.

You and I met in October on our return to school, but you went into Fourth 'A' and I into Fourth 'C'. Of the decent fellows, only Nanot remained in my class. Fortunately, Palaiseau and Bruneval also went to 'A'. I still had Ferrer, Cohen and The Twins to fear, but they no longer bothered about me. There is no need for me to go into details about those last years at Janson. I continued to be one of the best students, and the war had changed the relationships between the boys. My father was no longer a tramway employee: he was a soldier, and very soon a front-line soldier. He had spent 1915 in Villeneuve-Sàint-Georges, and we saw a lot of him, but at the beginning of 1916 he was transferred to a supply-depot near the lines. The day he told us of his departure, Maman had a terrible attack of nerves.

"I don't want you to be killed!" she cried. "They will kill you!"

My father assured us—I do not know whether he believed it, or whether he was merely trying to set our minds at rest—that the Ordnance Corps never took a risk. But Vinet the porter, who had had some experience and who was very pessimistic since he lost his leg at Charleroi, kicked the bottom out of this argument and threw us into despair. "The Ordnance Corps never takes a risk!" he scoffed. "Think again. Once they've massacred all the young ones like me they'll come for the old ones of your age. Otherwise why should they be sending you up there? What with their cannons and their *Taubes* . . ." My father treated him as a fool and they nearly came to blows. "That's right," Maman put in, "now start fighting, and in the meantime the Kaiser and Poincaré will come to an agreement behind your backs." This was the first time I had heard her express such a thought. Previously she had believed it was right to fight all the same and that France was struggling for the freedom of the world; but from the day my father was sent to the front she became once more as much of a rebel as before the war, and in addition to that, thoroughly gloomy. When she spoke to herself at table and I could catch a few of the words, I heard her repeating: "They'll kill him. . . . I've already lost Henri, and now they'll kill him. They'll kill them all. . . ."

Her face seemed to have shrunk to nothing and her hair was greying fast. She now began to look like her mother, whom I had never known, but whose full-size portrait hung above my bed—an old woman with a very small wrinkled face, with the same hard eyes and straight hair. During one of his leaves towards the end of 1917 she stayed up the whole night trying to persuade my father not to go back. She had been saving for nearly two years (I cannot think how) so that he could flee to Spain, Switzerland or somewhere. We could join him later. He shrugged his shoulders and said: "And do you suppose they would let me cross the frontier even if I gave up my arms? I still prefer to risk a bomb than to be certain of getting twelve bullets in me." Secretly I approved, as I did not want to leave Janson.

"Very well, you'll see, you'll see," she muttered. . . .

In 1918 Paris had air raids and Big Bertha. Despite the porter's remonstrances my mother never would take cover. I was a little frightened, but not unduly. When the sirens woke us up at night I went over my lessons while waiting for the All Clear. Maman sat at the table with her hands folded. She had grown into the habit of sleeping fully dressed, and no longer bothered to turn down the bed. Once I ventured to say to her that as she had no intention of leaving the room she might just as well sleep between the sheets. Her only comment was. "They're not going to find *me* naked!"

With the summer came the final examinations for graduation. I remember that I looked for you at the Sorbonne among the pupils from Janson. I met Fournier and learned from him that you were ill in the Midi. I thought I was luckier than you. I graduated, but Cohen and Ferrer were ploughed. When I told Maman of my success she merely shrugged her shoulders, so I wrote to my father. I remember his reply on a field postcard decorated with little flags: *I am very pleased to hear the good news, my son. I've told all the boys and we drank your health.*

I kept that card, and my lawyer read it out at the trial (he thought he was entitled to ferret about in my belongings). And then a week later, on my return home after a long walk as far as St. Cloud, my head full of future plans for my next exams and good jobs to follow, I found Maman sitting as she used to during the night raids. Before her on the wax table-cloth next to her work-basket was a crape band. Without stirring, she said to me, "Give me your jacket." I never disobeyed her orders. She placed it on her knee, and after looking at one sleeve and then the other, began to sew the black band round the left one. "Your father is dead," she said curtly.

I read the letter she had just received. Father had died

gloriously at his post on August 13th, 1918, in the railway depot at La Veuve (Marne) from an enemy bomb. Killed outright. My mother went on sewing the armband and murmuring: "*La veuve* . . . the widow . . . What will they invent next?" She did not cry, but sniffled each time and made a grimace. I would have liked to throw myself into someone's arms, to call out for my father and tell him that he should not be dead; but as Maman did not weep I did not weep either, at least not then. I sat down and watched her sewing. When she had finished she stood up and opened the wardrobe. Taking out a pair of my father's trousers, she flung them at me across the length of the room. "Here you are!" she cried. "You always wanted a pair of long trousers." I let them fall on the floor and threw myself on the bed, sobbing. "Well, what's all the fuss about?" said my mother. "You should have stopped him going back. Now he's dead. He's dead," she kept repeating the whole evening as she prepared the dinner as usual. Today I understand why she was not surprised. For years she had been expecting this to happen.

But on the following day she could not get up. She was delirious and shivering with fever. She called me Henri—my brother's name. I had never known her ill before, and I thought that she was going to die too. I went down to the porter's lodge. Madame Vinet came up and put cold compresses on her head and sat with her, while I went downstairs to keep Vinet company in his lodge. My future was decided there, Denis. I can see the pair of us now in that cave half-way between the ground floor and the first where the gas burned the entire day. Vinet kept running his hand over his wooden leg, and this caress sent shivers down my spine. He might have been between thirty and thirty-five, our age now; but at that time he appeared to me like an old, worn-out man, just as I must appear today to the little chambermaid. He declared that Maman must rest after such a shock and that her pension would not be enough to keep both of us without working. "So I shall have to leave school," I said. "You certainly will," he replied. Since the previous night I had lived in a state of complete coma with the feeling that there was no end to the misfortune that had fallen upon us–upon myself. It had all been too wonderful: the graduation, the Sorbonne and my dreams. But for my father I should never have gone to Janson. Naturally now he was dead I had to leave.

The children are still playing in the garden. Someone whom I did not notice in my preoccupation with my memories brought them slices of bread and jam. The hotel keeper's little boy has gone. Will their destinies change too, once they have lost their father? I am not worried about that. A fine inheritance awaits them from all the money that has been stolen right and left. They will go to high school. . . . They may even have private tutors so that they can remain in the country, which is more healthy. And they will have their mother's kisses, too. . . .

The doctor came during the afternoon and said that Maman had meningitis and insisted upon her being removed to hospital at once. She was taken away to the Pitié in an ambulance. I was not allowed to go with her as there was room only for the nurse. I remained alone for the first time in my existence. I wept like an imbecile for I don't know how long. Then I set out for the hospital. I had to cross the whole of Paris, but despite my frail appearance I was a good walker and not frightened of long distances. Before leaving I put on the trousers that Maman had flung in my face the night before. I thought they would make me look more serious and the the people at the hospital would look upon me as a man. They were right as regards length, but the belt! I had to take it in with safety pins.

They would not see me at the hospital. Visitors were allowed only on Thursdays and Sundays from one to three. I wanted to be certain at least that Maman was still alive. I wandered through courtyards full of wounded soldiers on crutches, with bandaged heads and arms in slings: some of them were laughing and joking with the nurses. People hurried by in white overalls. I got lost, but at last managed to discover a gentleman sitting in his office in shirt sleeves, who told me after consulting his list: "Mme Gallon? Her card has just arrived: delirium caused by emotional shock. To be kept isolated under observation. Are you her son? Well, my boy, come back on Sunday during visiting hours and perhaps you will be able to see her."

I returned to Passy. The Vinets had finished their evening meal and offered me some bread and cheese. We spoke once more about the future. "We must hope your mother won't be there long," said Madame Vinet. I was at the end of my tether. I did not sleep a wink all night. I could hear my parents whispering in bed and saw my father in his nightshirt crossing the room to drink out of the water-jug, which he often used to do in the summer.

Next Sunday at the hospital I went down the corridor as far as my mother's door and was able to speak to the nurse, but was not allowed to see the patient. The following Thursday they opened the door and I caught a glimpse of her. She was asleep in a little white room with an ice-bag on her head next to another woman who was groaning and clutching the iron bars of her bed. The second Sunday, the nurse told me that unless things improved they would be taking Maman away to the cemetery, to la Salpêtrière.

I went to the hospital every day. I used to stand in front of the grille for a long time wondering whether I was disturbing people, and then I would go despondently home.

I lunched with the Vinets. I wanted to pay them for the

money they spent on my account, but I did not know where Maman had hidden her savings. So in return for their kindness I swept the staircase every morning, and at night I told them I was not hungry and went to bed supperless. I also cleaned our room very carefully so that when she returned she would find everything in order. From time to time I looked at my exercise-books, but this made me want to cry.

One night on my return from the hospital Madame Vinet announced that she had found something for me. I forgot to tell you that since her husband had returned home she worked during the day as a dressmaker: she was very friendly with her employers, whom she called her clients. She was quite a different character from Maman. She could not help being gay and laughing with people, and did not bother her head whether there was justice in the world or not. Before my father's death, Maman and she naturally did not get on at all well together. She never came up as her husband sometimes did; but this attack of meningitis had overwhelmed her, and she related it all to everybody, with full details about me and my studies and the necessity for finding me a job immediately. It appears that that day she had spoken about me to Mademoiselle Templier, a very nice rich old spinster, the sister-in-law of M. Bloch-Templier, the banker.

To write this name after everything that has happened! There is another name that I ought to have written already —the name of the man who lives opposite and whose children I can see playing. I have so much to tell you, but we have plenty of time, haven't we, Denis? He is not due to return yet, and I write very fast. Well, Mlle Templier recommended me to the charity of her brother-in-law. I could call immediately at his office in the Boulevard Haussmann.

I went there next morning. You probably know it. It is an enormous building opposite the *Printemps.* It was naturally the first time in my life I had ever set foot in a bank. The immense circular hall like a circus arena with dozens of tables placed close together, all the bank clerks' heads beneath their lamps, the noise of typewriters and voices made my heart thump and made me stop once I had passed through the revolving door. A large man in a blue livery asked me what I wanted. He wore the initials of the bank on his collar in letters of gold and the ribbons of the military medal and the *croix de guerre* on his chest. His left arm was missing. I did not dare to say a word, and handed him the visiting-card. He glanced at it: the name of Mlle Templier must have carried some weight. He said to me: "Directors' board-room, fourth floor. The lift next to the staircase." I had never been in a lift. It smelled of disinfectant and could carry ten people. A small lift-boy, also in blue uniform, operated it. As I passed each floor I saw, seated at a table, an attendant dressed in the same blue and decorated like the porter, and behind him a long corridor.

On the fourth floor it was quite different. An usher with white hair, in tails and a silver chain round his neck, stood by the door of a great room full of armchairs and hothouse plants. He took my card and told me to wait. I did not risk entering the room. How extraordinary everything appeared to me! In the bay window at the end of the room I could see one floor of the *Printemps* with mannequins and globes blazing with light, although it was daytime. There was hardly a sound. I wondered how I should have the courage to reply to M. Bloch-Templier's questions. I was frightened of losing my trousers, which were so loose; but all this did not prevent me from thinking: Would it ever be possible to become a bank director, having only passed the first stage of my exams?

After some time the usher returned with a slip of green paper in his hand and told me to follow him. We went down a little staircase and found ourselves in front of the blue-liveried attendant on the third floor. The usher handed him the green paper and said, "For M. Sarrazin," and left without saying a word to me. Then I followed the attendant in blue with the limp. I could not understand why M. Bloch-Templier had not received me himself. We stopped in front of a door marked 'Staff Manager'. My guide went in alone. Again I had to wait for a long time. When at last he reappeared he merely said, "Go straight in." I had to cross an office where two girls with waved hair were typing and then into M. Sarrazin's private office.

M. Sarrazin questioned me. He was a thin, elderly man with a bitter mouth and wore pince-nez. He spoke curtly, keeping his eyes fixed on the green paper which he had placed in front of him. I replied to each of his questions as well as I could. At last he telephoned several times. I do not know to whom, but certainly to underlings. Then he told me that the bank would take me on trial for a week. I was to be employed in the 'portfolio' section, and if I gave complete satisfaction I should earn seventy-five francs a month. With that he rang for one of the girls, who took me into the outer office and made me fill up a form in triplicate. There was a pleasant smell of perfume. I felt I was in another world.

The girl rang a bell and the limping attendant in blue reappeared. She gave him one of the forms I had filled up and asked him to take me to the portfolio section. I returned once more to the ground floor, to the circus where every table seemed occupied and where I should never have believed a free place could be found. A flap was lifted for me to pass from the clients' to the employees' side. I was taken to a gentleman who was working enclosed in a glass case—there were several of these glass cases scattered about among the tables. They were the offices of department heads. The portfolio chief had been notified by M. Sarrazin. As he examined my form he murmured, "Nice writing." He was dressed in black, and noticing my mourning band, added: "You have lost your father and I have lost my only son. Our country exacts great sacrifices of us."

I did not know what to reply. I simply said, "Yes, monsieur."

He frowned and called out to a tall, fair young man through the window, "Provost!" and handed me over to him.

You must forgive me for giving you all these details, for I could not possibly miss one of them. The porter, the lift, M. Sarrazin, the perfumed typist, M. Delaunay's glass case . . . You see, I had no *choice*. The wonder I had hoped for at Janson I now experienced as I entered the Boulevard Haussmann. But at the same time I was frightened. It's not possible, I said to myself. It can't last. At the end of the week they will tell me they don't need my services any more. They are giving me a week's charity. I did not know then that banks never give charity.

Why have I written this disagreeable phrase? What have I to reproach Bloch-Templier with? For having had confidence in me? For having rewarded my efforts far in excess of my services? Anyone else in my place would still have been the chief's right-hand man today. Anyone else, yes. Anyone else would have learned how to protect himself, and would not have remained a stranger, as I did, with that same barrier between him and the others, as at high school. And yet many of my colleagues came from surroundings as poor as my own; but they had adapted themselves. It was noticeable from certain of their gestures—their way of putting on their hats, of fiddling with a ring—and from certain objects. Yes, objects—a ring, a coloured pocket handkerchief, a cigarette-case. Those boys knew how to speak and jest and to wink at girls. They were cocksure and self-assured. That's it, self-assured. I never got the hang of it.

I remember the day I left the Boulevard Haussmann to join A.P., Ltd., Adams Process, Ltd., and I went down into the hall to say good-bye to M. Delaunay, my first chief. He at least, I thought, leaves his glass cage of an evening and rediscovers the world. I too am in a kind of glass cage, but I never leave mine. But even if I did think that, I was convinced that things would change this time. I left the bank with a smile on my lips. Auguste, the big one-armed porter, touched his cap and said: "We're sorry to see you leave, M. Gallon. But when we remember how we saw you arrive seven years ago we are proud of you."

I am hot. I miss the fresh air with this window perpetually closed. We had plenty of fresh air at Melun. The windows are always open in the workshops, and swallows fly overhead. Even in your cell at night you can open your window—naturally only if the warder allows it. Is it time to go for a walk? The children are still playing in the garden, and I don't want them to see me with my beard and my sickly air. But no, they are too busy and I cannot bear this any longer. . . .

(Some time later.)

THE MAID must have profited by my absence to close the shutters. I had to ring for her on my return. The darkness prevents me from writing any more. As for lighting up with the shutters open . . .

Opposite, the children have disappeared and everything is closed like yesterday evening. I was out of doors about twenty minutes. On leaving the hotel I took the little street which runs alongside the house and leads down to the Loire. As it descends very steeply the ground floor on that side is raised very high; there are even ventilators at soil level beneath the windows. I should have liked to cross the main road at the river side to get a better view of the whole house. I did not dare. I entered the main street opposite the bridge and climbed as far as the church square. A clock struck three gentle chimes, and then three more. Could it have been the Angelus at this time of day? Then the bell began to ring fast. The little upholstered door was half opened and several old women in black came out. I thought I could hear singing inside the church. I thought of his funeral. But that day they will open the two main sculptured doors. I envisaged the black and silver draperies with his initial on the escutcheons, the wax candles at the end of the church round the catafalque, and the crowded nave filled with inhabitants from the town who will come to pay their last respects to one of their most eminent citizens killed by an unknown assassin.

I should have liked to go as far as the cemetery to see the path he would take on his last journey, but I did not dare to ask for such a piece of information. He has doubtless bought his plot in the churchyard, for he is a provident man. His widow will erect a monument to him—perhaps a plaque with a bronze medallion. His large face with those terrible small eyes will continue to dominate his world, and the maid will come and polish it with a bristled brush and harness soap. On All Saints' Day his children will bring flowers.

And I? What do they do with murderers? As no one will claim my body (Don't be foolish, eh, Denis? And above all don't waste any money to ensure a decent resting-place for my corpse!), shall I rot in a pauper's grave in B——? Or haven't I the right to be buried in certain cemeteries in some town reserved for condemned men and lepers? I shall never know and I don't care a ——. In any case I shall have ceased to exist. I should like my end to be like my father's. I never told you, did I, that nothing remained of his body? His sergeant-major, who came shortly after the Armistice to tell us how he died—he lived in the rue l'Annonciation three houses away from us—had already written to us, "The bomb probably fell right on top of him." They never found a trace, not even a button from his tunic. A good example, you see. And as there is every chance that when Maman dies she too will be buried in a pauper's grave, where she may already have been for some time now, farewell, farewell to the Gallon family! For I did belong to a family. Incredible!

As I walked my arm pressed this bundle of confidences against my chest, for I had put it in an inside pocket of my overcoat. It is ridiculous to wear an overcoat in this heat, particularly tonight when a storm seems imminent and the sky is full of black clouds. But these papers would never have gone into my jacket pocket. Nobody took much notice of me except the barber. He stood at the door of his shop, and when I passed by he drew back as if to let me enter . . . with such a look at my beard! There was not very much light, but I thought it better not to stay out too long. I bought *Le Matin* at the tobacconist's, which struck nobody as peculiar. It was to occupy me at dinner.

Until then I still have time to write to you a little. You know of my beginnings in the bank. At midday I did not go back to the rue de l'Annonciation as I had no money for the tram, so I walked round the Place de l'Opéra until two o'clock. I did not care in the least that I was hungry. I wanted to think over this extraordinary morning. I said to myself that Maman would be very pleased I was working. It was a Wednesday. Naturally I could not go to the hospital on Thursday and had to wait for Sunday.

The Vinets were delighted. I explained my work to them, a very simple job of endorsement and filing, and felt very proud of myself because they did not understand much about these things. From that day on, Madame Vinet gave me a sandwich or some bread and cheese every morning which I took to work with me. Most of the employees lunched in the bank restaurant. I pretended I was going home, and walked as far as the Trinité and ate walking up and down in the little street behind the church. I came to the Boulevard Haussmann in the morning on foot and returned on foot in the evening.

On the second day Madame Vinet remarked that we ought to pay a visit of thanks to Mlle Templier, so on Sunday morning she took me to see her client. An apartment, Denis! In the rue Scheffer, in a palatial house with marble, mirrors and a lift. Mme Vinet said to me, "As a dressmaker, I have the right to go up the main staircase." I remembered the back stairs of which Maman spoke so often with her little bitter laugh, and suddenly realized that Mme Vinet belonged to another world than ours, despite her porters' lodge and her husband. In addition to this she always wore a hat, whereas my mother never went out except bareheaded. That Sunday I noticed that she had powdered her face, and I found her pretty. I did not look at her for long, for after the waved and scented typists of M. Sarrazin I did not dare to look at women any more.

Near the bridge, just now, when I saw the main street spread out before me with the church and its two towers at the end, I thought of Mlle Templier. There was nothing particularly odd about this, for at the moment my head is full of such memories, but it was for another reason. Since the visit in question I have never been able to stop in front of a church without thinking of her. She opened the door to us herself. She was dressed in a nurse's costume and had a missal and a handbag in her hand. "I was just going out," she said.

Our visit did not last long. The three of us remained standing in the hall. She asked me a few questions just as M. Sarrazin had done, and her piercing eyes made me want to hide myself. She was tall and dried up with a long, wrinkled face. Her veil covered all her hair and not a single strand was to be seen. Mme Vinet had warned me: "You'll see. She looks like an old horse, but there's nobody better in the world." For the first time in my life I met a woman who was generous as she was rich, and I felt very surprised. At the end of her interrogation she gave me a sharp look and said, "A boy like you shouldn't bite his nails." Then she opened her bag and handed me a five-franc note. I did not want to take it, and she looked annoyed. To encourage me to make up my mind, she said: "You can take something to your mother. And now," she added, "good-bye. I mustn't be late for church. For thirty years I've always walked. I hope you will never fail to carry out your duties as a good Christian."

Mme Vinet replied quickly for me, "Of course not, mademoiselle."

"You must pray," said Mlle Templier. "Particularly now.

Pray that we may be given victory and that the war will soon be over."

We left. I was never to see her again. She died two months later.

In the street I asked Mme Vinet why she had lied. She shrugged her shoulders. "It didn't cost anything to give her a little pleasure." I dared not reply, but I was ill at ease as I remembered her piercing eyes. I began to look at the passers-by to see if they were carrying missals or not. I asked Mme Vinet if she ever went to church, and she replied with her gay laugh, "Of course I do–to keep in with my clients." I laughed a little too, until my embarrassment returned and I thought one should not deceive a person like Mlle Templier. After that we spoke of what I could take to my mother with the five francs. It was a large sum of money for us at that time. Finally we decided to wait until Maman was better.

That afternoon, on the way to the hospital, I went into a church, but I shall never know which one it was. I was trembling with emotion because I kept thinking that perhaps my father would know and curse me. Strange idea, wasn't it? For I believed in nothing. I had never been taught to believe, and in our house religion had always been considered an additional means of exploiting the poor. But I could not bring myself to admit that my father no longer existed anywhere, and I was under the impression that he was bound to be somewhere. You can explain that how you like. All I can say is that today a dead man appears to me dead as mutton, finished for ever, and I regret it because there ought to be a hell for certain people, even if I were obliged to roast in their company.

So for the first time in my life I entered a church. I did not know that it could be so dark and silent. It was pleasant there after the heat outside. There were a few people praying, but I discovered nothing, felt nothing–absolutely nothing.

And yet I can assure you that as I had flouted the shade of my father by crossing the threshold I was prepared for anything. "*Mon Dieu,*" I whispered, "do you exist?" I think it was a kind of prayer, but I got no reply.

On my arrival at Melun, when I appeared for the first time before the Governor, he asked me, after having studied my dossier and made a little speech about the prison, what my religion was. I replied, "None." He assured me that one always belonged to a religion even if one did not practise it. Do you think this is true? "Have you been baptized?" he asked. "No." "What about your father?" "It's possible." "Ah, you see," he said with satisfaction, and dictated to the warder who acted as secretary: "Catholic. Well," he added, "will you attend Mass on Sunday?" "As you like," I replied.

This answer nearly got me into trouble, and brought down on my head a lecture upon what he called 'the dangers of insolence': days of dry bread to begin with and then fines and solitary confinement. . . . "So, my agnostic friend, have you made up your mind to attend Mass?" At that moment I saw Mlle Templier in her nurse's uniform. Yes, mingled with the image which has not yet left my mind since the start of my affair I saw that holy woman, and replied, "No, sir."

If I had had faith, would I have led my life any differently? Led my life? Nobody leads his own life. And whether it be the fault of God or the Devil, two of us are going to die here and that's the end of it.

I went straight to the hospital from the church. The sister, who already knew me by sight, said: "Ah, there's been a change. You haven't been here for a week." I saw by her smile that the news must be good. My mother was no longer delirious and had left the isolation ward. I found her lying in a great corridor in one of a number of beds around which visitors were sitting or standing. Everything was white—the walls and the sheets—and sunny, and yet the impression was one of sadness. Perhaps because of the visitors, who, like myself, wore dark clothes; or perhaps because of the smell and the faces of all those sick people. I thought of my magnificent bank, of the lifts and the attendants' uniforms. Yes, I who had been ashamed of my father's uniform admired that livery. That was because I already saw it from above and was not a son of theirs.

Maman was lying back on her pillow looking around her. When she caught sight of me I think she smiled for a brief second. She let me kiss her on the forehead. I told her at once that I had given up my studies and was working in a bank. When she heard this she frowned, but made no reply. She had not opened her mouth since my arrival, and I began to be afraid. At last she asked in a voice which seemed tenser than ever, "How did you get hold of that idea?" After I had told her the story of Mme Vinet and Mlle Templier (I did not mention my Sunday morning visit or the church), she turned her head away and, fiddling with a button of her nightdress, muttered, "So there you are, living on public charity!"

"Not at all," I replied angrily. "I'm earning my living, and as a proof . . ." I took the five francs I had been given that morning from my pocket. Maman looked at the notes and suddenly appeared very tired. She closed her eyes and murmured: "All right, all right. We'll talk about it later. I want to get out of here." All of a sudden she opened her eyes and sat up in bed. I thought she was going to start screaming again as on the first morning of her illness, but she fell back on her pillow and began to cry softly. "My poor *Vieux* . . . my poor *Vieux*," she sobbed. Of course, I still did not count for her, and she was thinking of my father. I put the five francs down on the bed without her noticing, but she must have realized I was going to leave, for she said, "Bring me my woolly."

(*Evening.*)

THERE WAS a knock on the door just now and it gave me a terrible fright. When I am writing to you like this with the shutters closed, and particularly when I speak of my mother, I have only the past around me—the past and the image. I was frightened as last night. It was the little chambermaid again who had come to tell me that my dinner had been waiting a long time. I locked my writing-pad in the chest of drawers. As long as I don't leave the house . . . But I was in a hurry to get back to my room. The large table was empty this evening and the maid would have liked a little chat, but I buried my nose in *Le Matin.* I pretended to be reading, but did not actually read a line.

The following Sunday saw me at the hospital again. The evening before, M. Delaunay, my chief, had told me that as the result of his favourable report to M. Sarrazin I was to be taken on. I wanted to tell my mother this, but she did not give me a chance to speak. Without even replying to my greeting, she said, "You'll have to make up for lost time." I immediately thought she was cured! She had recovered her voice and her gestures. The first thing she did was to return my five-franc note with the remark: "I don't want your earnings. You owe the Vinets money. Pay them back." She had written out a list of commissions on a piece of paper: to fetch work for her from the hosiery in the rue de Passy, to see if the people with whom she used to work had gone on holiday or had found someone permanent to replace her. When she had finished she said, "You can go now." A nurse who had been watching us from the far end of the dormitory joined me in the corridor. She looked at me with a smile and murmured, "She's a great character, your mother, you know." She was young and pretty and I thought she was making fun of me. Once in the street I wondered why my father had had to die instead of my mother.

When she returned home a fortnight later she seemed to have been away for months. During this time I had formed my own habits of trotting between the Vinets' lodge and our empty room. With my job at the bank I felt a different person and no longer a little boy. After five minutes I had lost everything again, but at the same time my hatred had increased a hundredfold. I had abandoned high school and my studies to help my mother so that she could take it easy, and yet it all counted for nothing. She had not changed at all, although I had upset my whole life for her. The entire time at the hospital, even during the last few visits, I had told myself I must keep calm, but now when we were together . . . We saw each other only at dinner, for I only had time to swallow my coffee before leaving in the morning (however early I got up I always thought I should be late), and even that was too much. I felt as if I had a lump in my throat and could not swallow. "If you're not hungry," Maman said, "don't eat it. I'll heat it up tomorrow." I remember one piece of meat coming to the table three times in succession. Of a morning I found the coffee heated, but she never gave me anything to take with me for lunch, and I still got something from the Vinets.

Mme Vinet was absolutely furious, and kept saying to me: "And I who looked after her like a mother. Not even a word of thanks. Anyhow, what I do, I do for you!" Every day she gave me my little lunch-packet. She abused Maman in terms I found surprising, coming from her, and which distressed me. "Just wait," said Vinet, "I'll have a few words to say to that woman." But as he made this remark without stirring, stroking his wooden leg, I did not take him too seriously. One night when I climbed upstairs

I heard excited voices coming from our room. Vinet was shouting: "You're an old tramp! Everybody knows you're an old tramp!"

I began to tremble as I used to do when my parents quarrelled. My mother's harsh voice replied: "That's right, take advantage of my having no one to stick up for me. Go on, go on." I opened the door and said with downcast eyes, "M. Vinet, leave Maman alone." He came over to me, lifted my chin brusquely and replied: "Well, I'm —. Next time you can defend yourself." He went out, banging the door. I sat down. The sweat was pouring down my back. I wanted Maman to say, "How brave of you," but she stood there on the other side of the table. We could hear Vinet stumping down the stairs. "Defend yourself against whom?" she said at last with a jeer, and then added: "Dinner is ready. The young gentleman is served."

Another few weeks passed without our exchanging a word. I did not dare to visit the Vinets any more and bought just enough to satisfy my hunger at lunch. It was September and I had already seen several of my old comrades in the street who must have started higher maths or philosophy. I avoided all of them. One evening as I returned home I found Maman waiting for me, her shawl over her shoulders despite the heat, and a large bundle at her feet. She told me that she was leaving for good; that quite rightly I detested her because she despised me; that I was a bad son and would realize it one day, but that she had no need of any repentance; that she was leaving me without the slightest remorse because I was in good health and earning my own living. On the contrary, she did not wish to risk being a burden to me, that she had no fear on my account because in the circle I had chosen one could always rely on one's masters, provided one was a good dog, and she knew I would always be a good dog.

I have never seen such a performance. Maman did not raise her voice, but spoke as if she were reciting a lesson; and I stood there accepting everything she said, feeling completely overwhelmed as on the night when she blew out the lamp. I thought of that while she was speaking. Do you think she expected me to say something? Yes, obviously, just as I expected her to the day I dismissed Vinet. One realizes things when it is too late. "I'll carry your things downstairs," was all I said, a reply not to be particularly proud of. She replied in turn with her little leer, "Keep your strength for other people," and went out, leaving me alone in the room repeating to myself, Now I have no parents.

The Vinets came up almost at once. They had seen her pass their window with her bundle and had guessed she was leaving. They began by commiserating with me and abusing her, but I stopped up my ears without their noticing. Mme Vinet left the room to tell the story to the other tenants, who nearly all came to see what was happening. Normally they never came in because they were afraid of Maman, and I knew them only by sight from having passed them on the staircase. Within five minutes the room was full of people. They began talking among themselves, examining every object and the blank spaces on the walls. I noticed that Maman had taken away the photos of Grandmother and Henri, and then I said to myself: I want to leave too. I don't want to live in this house any longer. It's unlucky.

The rent had been paid up to the first of October. The Vinets thought it quite natural that I should go and live nearer the bank, particularly as I had no need of a kitchen or such a large room now I was alone. So I left with what little linen I possessed, my books and exercise-books and my father's clothes–two large packages. Turcas, an old chauffeur friend of Vinet, drove us (my first ride in a taxi) to a furnished apartment house in the rue de Provence which I had spotted the night before. I left the two cupboards, the chairs, table, the bedding and the kitchen utensils in case my mother came to claim them. Mme Vinet had said, "In the meanwhile, we'll let it furnished."

The furnished room in the rue de Provence seemed to me hardly habitable, but everywhere else had been either too expensive for my means or else they had refused me under the pretext that they did not want any trouble with minors. Here, on the contrary, the proprietress, a tall fat moustachioed woman, had looked at me more in a motherly way—motherly! And when I told her that I was employed in a bank she addressed me as *monsieur.* On the following day when she saw me arrive in a taxi, with an old chauffeur who treated me familiarly and offered me an *apéritif,* she said to me with a wink, "You know your way around, don't you?" The ignoble creature!

You may well wonder why I did not resume my studies at this juncture. First, I had not the means, as I had only my out-boarder's grant and I had to eat, but I think that had I suddenly been given the possibility of returning to Janson I should have refused. Now that my mother had left I began to realize that I had sacrificed nothing for her at all. I loved my bank and dreamed about it, do you understand? To be rich, to *deserve* to be rich! And I told myself that the quickest way of achieving this was in the place where one handles money. I dreamed of the commercial bills that passed through my hands and the discount calculations that were entrusted to me.

I could not wait to get to my desk mornings and afternoons. I looked upon the chairman as a god. He never appeared in the hall, but I imagined him to be tall and dry with a long, wrinkled face like Mlle Templier. A ridiculous portrait, as she was only his sister-in-law. His car was always parked in the rue Auber at the back of the building—a huge black Rolls driven by a chauffeur, who also wore military decorations. I often walked slowly in the hope that M. Bloch-Templier would come out of the bank at that moment and get into his car under my very eyes, but I dared not stop, for I was frightened I should be asked why I was loitering there.

I must tell you one more thing about my mother. How right she was! I have only thought that since I have begun to write to you. In 1925 when I entered the A.P., Ltd., that is to say seven years later, I felt a desire on Sunday to see the rue de l'Annonciation again. For no particular reason, but just to see it! At first I passed two or three times in front of the house, and then climbed the staircase to the porter's lodge. Vinet was still there under the gas-jet smoking his pipe. We had a drink together and he told me that he found me little changed—a little more saucy, perhaps, and a little better dressed. After that he confided his worries to me. He was very resentful about his *pension*, and more so now that there were four of them. They had had two more children. Mme Vinet, who had not changed either and who kissed me several times, was carrying the youngest. "Yes," she said, "you see the family has increased. We're looking for another lodge. Here we all have to sleep in the same bed, and it's unhealthy." We spoke of one thing and another—the housing shortage, my job and the people who had taken our room upstairs—a cinema operator and his wife.

My mother had never called for her furniture, and the Vinets had profited by letting the room furnished, ever since. Suddenly Mme Vinet cried: "Ah, but I've got something for you! A letter from your Ma." She stood up and began fumbling in a sideboard drawer. I felt a pang in my heart. For seven years I had scarcely given a thought to my mother. While searching among her papers, Mme Vinet explained that this letter had come about a month after I had left. As they did not know where to find me, they had opened it. My mother had simply given me her address. That was all. The Vinets had asked Turcas, the chauffeur who had helped me move; but that old drunkard could not even remember the name of the street, so they had waited for me to turn up. "Here it is," said Mme Vinet at last. I read:

My dear son, if it interests you I am living at 32 rue Clavel, Belleville, your mother.

I can still see this note and remember the very feel of it—ruled paper and written in violet ink. She must have wanted her furniture, I thought. After seven years it is better to give no sign of life. Imbecile. I know now what she wanted. Everything becomes clear when it is no longer of any importance. What grief I must have caused her! I stuffed the letter in my pocket and said, "Good, good!" The judge found this paper in my house. I left the Vinets my address in case something else should come for me.

I was living then in the rue de l'Isly, in a house not quite so horrible as the one in the rue de Provence. I had left, or rather I had run away from, that one not because of the dirt alone, but for reasons I will explain to you. I really must bring some sort of order into my memories. . . . First of all to sum-up my time at the bank and my entrance into A.P., Ltd. If I gave you every detail I should never finish (that Armistice Night, for example, when I wandered about the boulevards among a delirious crowd and felt so lonely, like a lost child, thinking of my father). I must hurry on, I must speed it up—this is already the third evening.

At the beginning of 1919 M. Bloch-Templier, in conjunction with certain of his fellow bankers, founded a professional school for bank employees. This, it appears, was an old idea of his which he had developed in a series of articles. The end of the war allowed him to realize this project. We were asked in each department for a list of those who wished to take these courses. Naturally I put my name down immediately. A few others followed suit, but only a small minority. The older men considered it useless, and most of the young ones could not be bothered to 'flatter the boss'. Flattery never entered my head: I wanted to get on, that was all.

The courses took place on the top floor of our building in the restaurant twice a week in the evenings. They were inaugurated by M. Bloch-Templier in person. The tables had been taken away to make room for rows of chairs. The hall was full to bursting-point and there were many employees from other banks. In the front rows sat our shareholders with the directors, inspectors and department heads. I hid myself right at the back of the hall.

When M. Bloch-Templier appeared on the rostrum the first rows applauded loudly, followed by the rest of the hall. He made a little sign with his hand, sat down and began to speak. Despite his figure, he bore no resemblance at all to his sister-in-law, for he had the body of an athlete, a moustache and grey hair. He did not speak long enough for my taste. . . . He spoke so well, in the direct and authoritative manner of a man used to giving orders—a real chief!

On several occasions I thought he was looking at me, and I drew myself up instinctively. He spoke to us of the great principles of banking—honesty, care and accuracy. He showed us that our profession was at the same time a science and an art, that one should not be in a profession like ours without understanding it, and above all without loving it, 'for love is an aid to comprehension', etc. Each one of us 'carried a field-marshal's baton in his knapsack more surely than any soldier'.

He quoted his own case as an example. He had begun in the *Comptoir d'Escompte* with the most humble tasks, more humble even than mine, at the very bottom; but he had worked and acquired knowledge. And now he wanted to help us to acquire knowledge so that we could rise more quickly than he had done. More quickly! I saw myself at thirty managing director of the Bloch-Templier bank. If anyone had told me that at thirty years of age I should have been for three years No. 9425 in a prison . . .

We must not confuse the issue. At the moment I am describing to you a good little boy—but when did I cease to be one? That is the crazy thing about it, Denis. I have never ceased to be one, I swear to you, or else I should have been able to protect myself. Well, never mind. I followed the courses in the certainty that my whole life depended upon it. They lasted two years (during which time, moreover, I had been given a rise because they were pleased with me in the 'portfolio', and this on top of my normal increase of salary to offset the rise in living costs), one year's elementary and one year's advanced course. The department heads and the inspectors, either ours or from other banks, were our teachers. In the second year we were even given a professor from the School of Political Economy.

That year was a delight to me. We studied everything concerning banking risks, commercial law, international law, and litigation, and M. Poder, one of our most efficient inspectors, put us on our guard, with a score of illustrations, against the possibilities of fraud. He initiated us into the mysteries of inspection. I have always been a very fast writer: I harvested the maximum amount of notes and learned them by heart in the evenings. I imagined myself sleuthing dishonest employees with all the ardour of a setter. "Like a dog," my mother once said; but I did not think of that then, and if I had thought of it I should not have understood.

At the end of the course the pupils had to pass an exam with a view to receiving a diploma. Obviously I went in for it. And I, the youngest and most insignificant, got the best marks. To distribute the awards, M. Bloch-Templier organized a session almost as impressive as his inauguration ceremony. He was in the chair as on the other occasion—I had not seen him again during those two years—and I was the first to receive from his own hands the diploma in question. A strange thing: none of the other diplomas had been won by our establishment.

I was told later that M. Bloch-Templier was extremely disappointed with this failure, but as at the same time one of his own employees had won the first prize, I imagine he wanted to give everybody a lesson at my expense: to the directors of other banks, to show them how they ought to treat their employees with school diplomas, and to shame his own employees while inciting the new students to work harder than their predecessors. I was therefore given another rise, which was not bad for a boy of eighteen, and M. Bloch-Templier decided that I should make the round of the bank—that is to say, a period in each branch so as to have practical experience in what I had learned at the lectures.

This stage lasted until my military service. On my return I was to be transferred according to my capabilities to some particular branch with a chosen position. All this I learned publicly from M. Bloch-Templier's own lips as I received my diploma. I was trembling with confusion.

Normally the tour of the bank was reserved for upper-class boys who were taking very advanced exams to be financial inspectors or to step into their fathers' shoes. And you have to work! You remain for months on end in each branch undisturbed. But all the same . . . It appears that bankers sometimes lend their children to each other for this apprenticeship. Thus we had with us Jean Raphaël-Ambert, who later became manager of Ambert, Raphaël-Ambert & Co. A nice boy, Denis, rather the same type as yourself, very genial and frank, never giving the impression that he was heir to a few millions. He was just finishing his tour when I began mine. He spoiled everything for me, though he certainly never realized it for a moment. Whenever we met he always said something pleasant to me, and once, despite his age and position, asked me for some information which I was able to give him. He spoke *in my favour* at my trial. But what could you expect? His mere presence in the establishment under the same conditions as myself only revived my agonies of Janson.

Once more I felt myself a pauper admitted on sufferance among the rich. Outwardly the position was no longer the same, of course, for here I was 'the boss's darling'—rather as if at Janson I had been sponsored by the headmaster. The department heads were well disposed and pleased with my attitude and efforts, but the juniors turned their backs on me. They would have rubbed their noses in the dirt for a Jean Raphaël-Ambert in the hope that they might one day get a job in his bank or benefit by the fact that he might work here after his father, who was on our board of directors. Whereas I . . . But perhaps I did not know how to behave, and harbour hidden motives. In short, I began to be alone once more.

Before I obtained my diploma in 'portfolio' I often laughed and joked with the others. One of them, Provost, who had been detailed to show me the ropes, had taken me out to lunch two or three times. He took me to the cinema on my seventeenth birthday, and one day did me a really great favour. I'll tell you about it. I still continued to be friendly with him up to the time when I started my tour of the bank, lunched next to him upstairs in the restaurant and went over to say good night of an evening. I could, perhaps, have confessed to him that I suffered from the attitude of the others, but I had not changed and I should never have dared to complain, particularly now that I thought people were jealous of me. Well, because of my silence and because of the story I am going to tell you, I lost even Provost.

The wind is rising. It is making the damper in the chimney rattle. I predicted there would be a storm when I went for a walk just now. How smart of me to have noticed this noise! I had grown almost calm this evening, almost at home. If this wind continues I know it will become intolerable as on my bad nights at Melun when it blew in the tree-tops and against my window overlooking the Seine. One morning after a sleepless night I asked the chief warder if I could have some cotton wool for my ears, otherwise I should go mad. "Do you think you are in a lunatic asylum?" he replied, "Go crackers first, and then we'll see afterwards."

Did I go insane? Not then. I had no idea before my little experiences there what powers of resistance my carcass possessed. When I think that I was rejected as unfit from the Army! Six years of confinement, seventy-two months, plus fourteen on remand. A long time, you must admit. There are some who cannot bear as much as that, and go mad or kill themselves. Admittedly I have grown thin, but I lasted the course all the same. Because of an image—no, an idea, the idea which brought me here. Yet isn't one insane to be determined to carry through such an idea to the end, no matter what the cost?

More futile questions? It's the fault of that damper. I will wedge it with a piece of paper. That will be one less noise.

THE STORY I have to tell you concerns perhaps the first youthful experience that I understood immediately because someone took the trouble to explain it to me, but I reaped nothing but sorrow from it as I did from all the others. I had just been transferred to Foreign Exchange, and on the first evening M. Gauthier, the head of the department, told me to check the cash in foreign currency. This did not amount to very much, for the bank had only small dealings in specie: in their foreign business transactions our clients usually demanded either cheques, transfers or letters of credit; and when they travelled took only enough local currency to cover their travelling expenses—tips for the porters, as M. Gauthier explained to me when he gave me this task.

The clerk in charge of this cash was called Delsuc, a man of about thirty with spectacles, who did not even bother to greet me and went on writing while I began to check. From time to time, however, when I felt he was eyeing me, I looked up and smiled. He buried himself in his books once more without a sign of recognition. I was quite accustomed by now to this kind of reception in each new department I entered. I had before me a statement from M. Gauthier and some small bundles of notes. When I counted the dollars I found that they were thirty short. I rechecked them perhaps ten times, but there were still thirty short.

I wanted to point out this mistake to Delsuc, but at that moment he closed his books and went off to the lavatory. So I went to M. Gauthier and pointed out the mistake. He sent for Delsuc. I found him soaping his hands slowly like a man who is not thinking about what he is doing. He admitted to M. Gauthier that he had borrowed that sum on Saturday—it was now Monday—to pay the doctor who had been attending his daughter. He thought that he would be able to find the money on Sunday and replace the deficit on Monday morning. "Find the money?" said M. Gauthier. "Yes, from a friend," said Delsuc. "That won't hold water," replied M. Gauthier angrily. "You've been gambling." They both went to see M. Sarrazin.

The story soon got round the bank. At the end of the day when I went to the 'portfolio' to say good night to Provost, I noticed that he gave me a funny look. He reproached me for having spoken so quickly to the chief and said I should have given Delsuc a chance. I should have told him, for example, that I would wait until the following morning before handing in my figures, and I hoped by then that they would be in order. Delsuc would have understood and would have arranged, somehow, to replace the money. I had not been told during my courses how to act in a case like this, and I should never have been capable of thinking it out for myself. I was far too young and inexperienced. And even if I could have imagined such a thing I should have been far too scared of angering M. Gauthier not to have given him my figures the same evening. In any case, why hadn't Delsuc given me my cue? Why had he left just at the moment when I should have asked him about it? But this did not prevent me from feeling very unhappy at Provost's rebuke. "I'll apologize to Delsuc tomorrow," I said. "It'll be too late," he replied.

He was right. The following morning M. Gauthier told me that Delsuc had been dismissed on the spot and that he was lucky not to have been prosecuted. He had been made to sign a paper agreeing to pay back the thirty dollars within the week. I remembered the paper that Mme de Bimont wanted my mother to sign. Oh, I'm not making any comparisons. For Delsuc was a thief, and a thief with no excuse, a gambler. Yes, a man who steals to gratify some passion or other has no excuse. Lucky, as M. Gauthier said, not to have been prosecuted. We know some people who did not come off so easily, don't we? It is true it was only a matter of thirty dollars.

That is the story of Delsuc. From that day on I did not dare to approach Provost again, and I gave up going to the bank restaurant in order to avoid him. I relapsed into complete solitude and took my lunch in the little café where I usually dined just beneath the place where I lived. It was quite a different house from the one in the rue de Provence, and I must now explain to you why. You will see at the same time what a good fellow Provost was.

I told you how I originally went to the rue de Provence. If I had had my way I wouldn't have stayed there twenty-four hours because it was so filthy. I had to spend the whole of my first Sunday cleaning my room, the den they called a room. Our house in the rue de l'Annonciation had been poor, but my parents were spotlessly clean and so were the Vinets. But there, as soon as you entered the corridor you were overcome by the smell of damp, rancid fat and worse still . . . altogether enough to make you retch.

The landlady, Mme Mourgues, whom everybody called 'Old Mother Mourgues'—that abominable, revolting 'Mourgues'—had certainly never used a broom in her life. She spent her whole day in a room on the ground floor, which may have once served as the porter's lodge. She ate and slept there and watched the incomings and outgoings through a pane that opened in a glass door. She would not have any women in her hotel. "There are enough brothels in this quarter as it is," she used to say. The truth is that this filthy slattern with her moustache had no other idea except to go to bed with her lodgers.

The Gare Saint-Lazare brought her a great many soldiers who took rooms for the night. She offered herself to most of them, and the affairs finished the following morning with shouts and screams because these boys counted on not having to pay for their night after their sacrifice, whereas Old Mother Mourgues threatened to call the police, because she was as miserly as she was revolting. She had two or three of them arrested during my stay there. She got on very well with the police, who, instead of listening to the soldiers' stories, gave them a good beating to shut their mouths.

The few permanent residents had grown accustomed to these scenes and never batted an eyelid . . . all old men who had nothing to fear, or casual travellers, I don't know which. I never spoke to any of them, knew none of them by name nor what they did for a living. I only met them on the dark staircase and could hardly distinguish their faces. During the first few days one of them growled as he saw me: "Well, would you believe it? Young blood!" I did not yet know Mother Mourgues' propensities and thought he was merely referring to my age. I laughed a little, and the good man shrugged his shoulders and muttered, "Swine!"

After a few weeks I found things out for myself, but I had never for a moment thought that one day I might play the role of those brutes who spent the night on the ground floor. What a memory, Denis! The things that formed my life! Now that I bring them to light I wonder if I do not deserve a little pity all the same. There was always my cowardice, of course; but did the question of luck enter into it at all? I might quite easily have been accepted in another hotel just as modest but run by decent people like the Vinets, for example. Their lodge was more wretched than Mother Mourgues' room and never saw the light of day; and yet Mme Vinet was young and attractive, powdered her face and smelt nice.

Of course, I might have become a millionaire, the French Ambassador or the Archbishop of Paris. But here I am, a brave little future murderer and suicide, who lost his virginity at sixteen to a bearded woman. Charming, isn't it? She waited for nearly six months, during which time she contented herself with ogling me as I passed or murmuring some polite phrase. And then suddenly she began to call me 'my little sweetie' or 'my little mouse', and her eyes terrified me. Can you see them? They were the bestial eyes of frogs at spawning-time.

One evening when I had come home rather late–it was during the early part of my course–she invited me into her room on some pretext or other and locked the door behind her. I was terribly frightened. I wanted to scream, but could not open my mouth. My legs flagged and I had to sit down.

I'll tell you the whole scene, for it was unbelievable. That monstrosity undressing with feminine smirks, uncovering a body perhaps not so bad after all, but with that face and those smells and in that hideous, brightly lit room! I imagined people in the corridor peering at this spectacle through the chinks of the curtain that covered the glass door. And for the first time in my life I saw a naked woman: I could not take my eyes off that body and I was shivering with terror. Then what do you think she did? She seized a new bottle of eau-de-Cologne from the dressing-table and began to perfume herself–her armpits, her breasts, her belly. She must have bought it in my honour. Then she undressed me in turn like a child and dragged me down on to the bed. She did not have it entirely her own way. I began to struggle and resist. With one hand she lowered the lamp, which went out, and with the other pressed me close to her.

I opened my eyes wide in the darkness and tried to find some means of escape; but as I struggled I was afraid of hurting her, for I have always had a horror of violence, even more of giving blows than of receiving them. And then, once I could no longer see anything, I became aware of the contact of naked flesh and the perfume of eau-de-Cologne.

My terror suddenly gave way to something else. There you are! But when I had finished I was overcome with nausea and had to fight it back so as not to be sick. She fell asleep. I waited a long time, and then dressed in the dark, fumbled for the door-handle, opened the door and left.

It was almost midnight. I drank a coffee in a *bistro* to settle my stomach. Then I began to walk. I had to find a quarter where there was night life so as not to draw attention to myself. I went to the Halles and stayed there all night. I managed to arrive at the Boulevard Haussmann earlier than usual. I wanted to see Provost, not to speak to him, just to see him. But as soon as he came up to me he said: "What's happened to you? You've done something silly."

I think he must have guessed, so I told him everything in a few words, as I dared not remain silent. He told me that some pretty girl would soon efface this memory, that I was not to set foot in the rue de Provence again (I had already decided that myself) and that he himself would go at six o'clock and fetch my things.

That was the day he invited me to lunch for the first time in the bank restaurant. I was ashamed and thought that everybody would be able to read my nocturnal adventure on my face like Provost. But nobody paid any attention to me except those who knew me and said good morning. It was very pleasant with bunches of flowers on the tables and waitresses dressed in blue and white. A huge hall with tables for four or eight, where the wives of the married men could join their husbands. People chattered and the whole atmosphere was quite different and gay. I felt as though I had washed myself clean again. The heads of departments and inspectors lunched at reserved tables some distance away.

The shareholders and directors sat at the far end in a little private dining-room where the food was the same price. Some of them passed through our hall and acknowledged our greetings cordially. I had rediscovered my zest for living. What a curious period youth is, Denis! When, in order to be in harmony with existence, it suffices to lunch in a bank restaurant and to see an exchange of greetings between directors and employees!

That evening Provost left me in a café in the rue du Havre while he went to see Mother Mourgues. I felt less sure of myself than at midday and thought I should see her return with him to force me to go back to her hotel, and that I should follow her for fear of the police. But an hour later Provost returned alone with my packages. He shook his head compassionately and said to me, "My condolences!"

I could not even muster a smile. He told me that the old woman had said absolutely nothing when he had told her the object of his visit. She had simply gone up to my room with him to see that I had stolen nothing during the night while she slept. Like the rest of her lodgers, I had paid in advance, but she pretended I still owed her two weeks' rent. Provost paid it. Then she had watched him collect my things, making flattering remarks about his hair and calling him 'handsome boy'.

Provost took me to a little *bistro* in the rue de l'Isly where he knew the proprietor, and to avoid any formalities introduced me as his cousin. There were several empty rooms on the first floor and they gave me a very respectable one with electric light, and looking out onto the street. I could eat quite cheaply in the *bistro*, and the proprietor's wife was a very good cook. I soon forgot my appalling night with Mother Mourgues and began to lead a peaceful existence, fully occupied by my day's work and the evening courses.

As soon as I had been given a rise I lunched at the bank with Provost, but after the affair with Delsuc I never left the rue de l'Isly except for my work. I spent my evenings, Saturday afternoons and Sundays there. In four years I never once went for a walk on the boulevards, although they were only two yards away. Yes, once—the day of the Victory Parade. After my courses I went on studying at home. I tried to pass my Philosophy exam alone.

One afternoon I went to Janson in the hope of seeing you or Fournier come out and to ask you for your advice and your notes. I had hardly arrived in the rue de la Pompe when I realized that you must have finished your studies more than a year before. I bought a cheap second-hand manual of philosophy—the first book I ever purchased—and learned it by heart. I was never unhappy in my room, and felt lonely only in the bank when surrounded by other people. As soon as I was really alone and had buried myself in my book I forgot everything. It would not be true to say that I never thought of Maman. Sometimes I imagined she would come in, and heard her little laugh and quickly shut my manual; but knowing that she would not really come and put out the lamp, I no longer strained my eyes, and my heart beat with joy.

During the first few meals I exchanged a few words with the owners of the *bistro*, Monsieur and Madame Palois, or rather I answered their questions. They soon got tired of this, particularly as they were always busy. Taxi drivers, railway workers from the Gare Saint-Lazare and the prostitutes of the neighbourhood came regularly to drink a glass at the counter or to sit down for a snack. At the beginning they made all manner of jokes, because they saw that I lowered my eyes and blushed. They called me 'the little virgin'. If only they had known! But they soon left me in peace. I had nothing interesting to offer them, and besides, they came to the Palois' for a rest. The ones who sat down often took their shoes off under the table and talked of their troubles and their daily adventures: the two nearly always went together. At first these stories embarrassed me because they made me imagine things, but at the same time I listened with my ears wide open.

I soon grew *blasé*. One of them, however, whom they called Big Irma, had a way of telling stories. I dreamed about them in my room without her realizing it, and it was her fault that I started bad habits. I am telling you everything, Denis, as I am bound to do. In any case, it is no more shameful than hating one's mother. One day Big Irma did not turn up, and on the following day we learned that she had been run over by a bus just outside the station.

The wind has stopped blowing and I thought it was over; but no, that was a clap of thunder in the distance. The first storm of a summer that I shall not live to see. I wonder if it's going to rain. To walk in the rain once more–for the first time after so many years! I sometimes managed to catch a few drops, but never more, between the dormitories and the workshops at Melun. If it is raining tomorrow morning I shall go out, and people can think what they like. I shall invent some errand–a newspaper, a pencil or some paper to buy–for if I continue at this speed my writing-block will not last me.

How curious it is! Everything which comes into my head now runs straight into my pen. It is a way of thinking aloud. That is how people write books. A colleague, Denis, I offer you a new colleague, a slightly backward one, fortunately. I must confess to you that I did try to write in the old days, not at the time I am speaking of, but later–

after my military service and after my second period in the bank while I was with A.P., Ltd.

I thought of you a great deal then and made up my mind to send you my manuscript, but my attempt was short-lived. I threw everything into the waste-paper basket after twenty pages. But you have gained nothing by waiting all this time. It is no good my going quickly and leaving out a thousand things. I keep rambling, rambling.

Will he leave me time to finish? It would be too much if he reappeared before I finished my story, and you never knew more than you do now. 'A 650,000-franc swindle. The André Gallon Case, etc.' But now that the proprietors know about my work I can continue all night.

When I began to write to you I thought simply of explaining the affair, but as I go on I see that it is the result of my whole life. It's not a question of minimizing his responsibility: that would be the last ignominy. But all the same—I wish I knew how to express myself. I know of no other method except to tell you one thing after another.

In 1922 I went before my military board and was accepted despite some hesitation on the part of the doctor —another one I have to thank for nothing but misfortune. But naturally I could not suspect anything. I remember that while waiting my turn amongst many boys, naked like myself, I tried to think of my father, of his death and the war, and could think of nothing but the 'Mourgues' and Big Irma. When I left there, while the others were buying themselves cockades and bright badges to pin on their jackets or in their caps, I followed a girl. "If you have five francs," she said, "I'll let you see." I had five francs, but in front of her hotel I ran away.

In September I joined an infantry battalion, the 62nd Foot at Vannes. You, who were ill, did you have any experience of barrack life? From the moment of departure from the Gare d'Austerlitz I felt lost in this train crowded with boys who did not know one another and who immediately became friendly. I never closed an eye all night, for they played cards, emptied haversacks and bottles and roared obscene songs as we went through stations. I, who had never been in a train before in my life, was ashamed. How can I express it? I was ashamed of the vulgarity of the people, and I began to understand why I had been insulted at the *lycée* because I belonged to the plebs. At the same time I was furious at not knowing the songs they were singing, at not laughing with the others and at being out of my element.

I had been dragged almost by force into a compartment of boys who, like myself, had to get out at Vannes. The train arrived at five o'clock in the morning, and as we did not have to report until midday they all planned to take advantage of the darkness and to jump out on the lines and make a trip into town. One of them, a boy named Corfmat, who came from that part of the world, gave them all the necessary tips. When we got out of the train I found I was the only one of the group to report to the orderly-room. There were, however, other idiots in the train, for actually quite a lot of us reached the barracks. It was cold and dark, but the building was not far away.

That day! With nothing to do but wander about the courtyard for hours. Then we were given a questionnaire—the four military maxims and 'What are your impressions on arrival in barracks'? I could not write down what I thought, and put down anything that came into my head. We had soup in the mess-room. I remember the smell—no, perhaps I am mixing it up with the soup at Melun—the smell of cats and dish-water. Hideous despite the cleanliness. I had no knife, but was lent one by my neighbour Barrat, a grocer's boy who kept repeating all the time, "It's a fine life, isn't it?"

I was examined by the doctor, drew my equipment, went up to the dormitory with all that junk and then back to the square once more—like any young Frenchman of twenty. I noticed, however, that a lot of them continued to take things as a joke. For myself, I felt I had never known loneliness before, and that I had been transported into a world in which it was impossible to live. I understood less than nothing of what was going on around me—duties, guard relief and all the noise, the stables, the calls and particularly the bugles. When at last I went to bed in one of those beds that squeak every time you move and heard the bugle sound 'Lights Out', I began to sob like a child and call for my father. Silently, of course. The boys came back in the middle of the night completely drunk. I heard them vomiting.

The following day, after my hair had been shaved off and I had been given a regimental number—No. 4039—I thought, Here I am in prison. I had no idea . . . Nor did I have any idea that prison could have so little effect. I did not suffer either at the Santé or at Melun as I did during those first days in barracks. It is true that in gaol I no longer existed. I did not even know that one day I should decide on the plan that has brought me here (in any case I did not decide it in one day, for the idea came to me little by little, quite gently like a rising tide).

But prison or anything else then . . . They could have buried me alive and I should not have noticed it. Whereas at Vannes it was quite the opposite. I had left the Boulevard Haussmann very happy because I had finished my tour of the bank, and because on my return I hoped to enter 'Financial Intelligence'—M. Sarrazin had given me an inkling of this on the eve of my departure when he handed me a little bonus—that is to say, into the most select department, where, according to him, 'only the chosen few are admitted'. Therefore I looked upon conscription as a sort of long vacation before my real start as a model employee. I imagined that all this would be taken into account. And as you will see, it was taken into account a fortnight later. But at the beginning, in the recruits' quarters, with my shaved head, ill-fitting uniform, regimental number, the language used by everybody—the sergeant instructors, the corporal and the old soldiers—and 'Army Regulations', I thought everything was lost.

However, I had a success in the dormitory on the second day. So far I have never mentioned my games, Denis, for even I played occasionally when I was a child. Maman never allowed me to bring anyone home, and usually I preferred to amuse myself outside with my friends from the rue Chernovitz.

We played at Red Indians and at 'Cops and Robbers' or anything else; but when the weather was too bad and I was obliged to remain indoors, and of course if my father was there, I had my toys, or rather 'the' toys—a box of jigsaw puzzles which could be made into six coloured pictures of animals; four tin soldiers as big as skittles and a very small rocking-horse for a child of one or two. Henri's toys, which Maman had bought a few days before his death, because at that moment she would have bought anything.

My father always used the same tactics. "Perhaps Dédé might have the toys," he would say, and Maman took them out of the cupboard and put them on the table saying, "Take care of them." And if a soldier fell on the table-cloth or a piece of the puzzle fell on the floor she would take them all away again. "You're not going to break them for me." Then my father said, "Come, it's time for pack drill." This was my favourite game, because at least it was my own.

One Sunday when we were alone I asked Papa if he

played this game with Henri, and when he said, "No," I felt very happy. It was simply a question of making up a pack as in barracks and of making a perfect cube of the most heterogeneous objects—a blanket, a casserole, shoes and notebooks, Papa's cap or anything that came to hand. Maman shrugged her shoulders, but as she liked to see my father happy she left us in peace. We enjoyed ourselves, I assure you. I always retained my love for really well-made parcels, and when I left the rue de l'Annonciation my packages truly astounded the Vinets and old Turcas.

On the second day in barracks, therefore, after the first inspection, when we had to learn how to make our packs, I amazed everybody, including the instructor and the old soldiers, and I was treated as a 'bright boy'. Anyone else would have known how to take advantage of this, but I merely told them the truth. Do you know what they called me after that? The 'militarist's son'. It was a fool of an old soldier, Le Drehanno, who invented the nickname. I ought to have taught him a lesson, but I never said a word.

Let me get on with the story. After a fortnight, candidates for prospective corporals and sergeants were asked for. In the case of myself and a few others, thanks to our school certificates, the captain decided that we should take an examination for general education to see if we were suitable for commissions. The exam took place in the barracks and I was accepted. A day or two later a detachment of us was sent to a military school at Nantes. This gave me renewed courage, and in my new surroundings the impression of being a prisoner vanished.

The captain here did not call us *mes enfants,* as the old man did at Vannes. He was a young, very brilliant and distinguished officer and a war hero into the bargain. At his lectures he addressed us as 'gentlemen'. All my companions were educated and even cultured, many of them from universities and very much of the same stamp. I thought that I should make friends here. I had a great need of doing so, and naturally I was not capable. . . . It is not enough to wish: one must be able. . . . And I have never been able.

I have never got on well with people. With you? How do I know? You pitied me, and as you are intelligent you surrounded this pity with gentleness. But why should you find me particularly likeable? You did not know me. No one has ever known me. I do not pretend that even if they had they would have liked me very much. I am too convinced of the contrary. But at least once you do know—I mean after I've fulfilled my duty—perhaps you will find me worthy of a little respect. That would be wonderful.

Besides, at Nantes, the question did not arise for very long, for I could not last it out. The training was ten times harder than at Vannes. In addition to the courses, we were given the most trying tests; constant drill and exhausting route marches with full pack, grenades, ammunition and wearing gas-masks. No one who has not been through this can realize what it means. The whole platoon nearly passed out, but for the others a day's rest was enough to restore their vitality, and then, instead of resting, they trooped into town and enjoyed themselves. I lay on my bed and could not move. I grew thinner every day.

One morning on my way back from the racecourse where we did our manœuvres I fainted, and after the first month, in spite of all my efforts, I had to give up. The doctor did not hesitate a second. You cannot imagine with what regret I returned to Vannes. Once more in my life I felt repulsed and rejected, and this time entirely as a result of my own weakness. I could not understand what had happened. At the *lycée* I was quite passable at gymnastics, and I thought I was a good walker. Probably I already harboured the infection which had been suspected at my medical and which might have cost me my life.

On my return to the battalion I began to live a peaceful, futile life. Old Captain Cadio, the Commandant's adjutant, a fine man who was genuinely sorry for my misfortune, put me in the office as assistant quartermaster. I worked with the chief accounts sergeant, who was also a good fellow and who soon relied on me for all his book-keeping. There were no more classes. Twice a week, on Wednesdays and Saturdays, the 'bureaucrats' were given a little perfunctory drill on the barrack square. On Saturday this finished with a five-minute march-past with music and bugles. I saw my eighteen months passing like this. I met my fellow recruits in the mess-room or in the canteen and stood my drinks like the rest. Everyone was very pleasant to me and flattered me because they knew I was on good terms with the Captain, and instead of wangling leave for myself I put forward the requests of the others.

I did not leave Vannes the whole winter. Where should I go? I was not expected anywhere. During the whole eight months I received only one letter—a visiting-card from M. Bloch-Templier with a note in his own handwriting:

With thanks and good luck to the first diploma winner of our professional school.

in reply to a card I sent him for New Year. Beyond this, nothing. There were others who were in the same position. We walked the streets on Sundays. At the beginning I should have liked to know the history of the gates, the towers and the houses we passed on our walks, but no one else was interested in these things. And as it was perpetually raining we ended up in a café.

I learned to play cards and became a great expert at *manille*. The old soldiers initiated us into the brothels in the rue de la Tannerie and we went back there from time to time. One evening three of us went there together. The girls were not at all bad. One from the Tabarin, whom I chose on several occasions, certainly made up for Mother Mourgues. I once asked her to go out with me, but she said that it was not allowed. And then one day I met her in town with an artillery sergeant, and never returned to the Tabarin or elsewhere.

One Sunday—my only extravagance that year—I stood myself a boat trip to have a look at the sea. It was an old boat which plied along the gulf of Morbihan and put in at all the little ports on the coast and touched at the islands. Land was visible all round. The water was calm as a mill-pond, but we were on the high seas all the same. I was with two comrades who had brought their girl friends along and thought of nothing but flirting. I went and sat in the bows and breathed the sea air into my lungs. It was a cold sunny day and I enjoyed it so much that I wanted to weep.

When we arrived at Port-Navalo the boat began to rock. We were approaching the narrow entrance to the gulf, and I discovered the Atlantic with an emotion that I cannot describe to you. I should have liked to sail on, far, far away, till we were lost and vanished in the blue. The boat started on its return journey. I made a resolution to make several long sea voyages later on when I became rich—alone, of course, because I could not conceive then of ever being anything else. But what did solitude matter on the sea? Just another of those vows I shall never keep.

I have not even seen the Atlantic again. I remember that after I had been given a sentence of eight months' imprisonment I asked my lawyer if I should be sent to Devil's Island. It was an idiotic question, of course, but I had lived in another world since the beginning of the affair and they had told me so many times that I should receive the maximum penalty unless I made up my mind to speak. I always remember Maître Gaillard saying, "No," and my reply, "What a pity!" He did not understand. I was thinking of the sea and convicts escaping in a storm. Not that I should have wanted to escape myself, but I should have been close to the sea and could have seen it all. If ever you make a long sea voyage, Denis, think of me.

At the end of February an epidemic of 'flu decimated the town and the barracks. Men reported sick by thirties and forties every morning. It was my turn on the 12th of March. Aches and high fever. . . . "With the threat of lung complications," the doctor had declared. As the military hospital was full I was sent to the Hôtel-Dieu, which was for both men and women. I do not know whether it was the result of my exertions with the platoon or what, but a week later complications set in and I had a serious congestion of the lungs. A long series of cupping-glasses, camphor injections and hot baths. Despite all this I grew rapidly worse. I sweated so much that I had to have my sheets changed several times a day: I could not breathe, was delirious or fell into a death-like coma.

A fortnight later the doctors diagnosed a suppurating pleurisy with the necessity for an operation. When the doctor told me this news he asked me if I wanted my family notified. I replied with conviction that I had no one in the world. In my delirium I saw myself at the hospital where my mother was still lying in the little isolation ward and I was present at her end. My father stood next to me. We left the hospital together hand in hand, and he said to me, "We must go and buy two crape bands, and after we've had a drink we'll take her some flowers."

They performed a thoractomy—under anaesthetic, of course. Afterwards I was easier, but I suffered a great deal from the wound and the drain. To sum up, this illness, the only one I have ever had, taught me physical suffering. I was in hospital two months convalescing. During that time I sometimes thought of my mother, especially on visiting-days. My comrades came to see me, and the first time I went into the garden, Cassatte, the accounts sergeant I told you of, gave me his arm. As soon as I began to feel better I started to read: old newspapers and weeklies that were lying about and had been sent by charitable people to the hospital. Also a few very dirty books with pages missing—I found the same type at Melun—all sorts of popular novels and thrillers which did not amuse me because I could learn nothing from them, and six school editions. I devoured, for instance, *The Adventures of Télémaque*, and learned a whole handbook of anatomy by heart.

I continued to browse over my philosophy book which I had brought with me from Paris. Despite this, time passed slowly, particularly during the long June days. I wondered what would become of me. The season of summer manœuvres was approaching. I was better, of course, but I could not see myself starting platoon drill again. Without my having to ask, the doctor was of the same opinion.

On the 15th of June I was sent before a medical board at the Caserne des Trente. Five minutes' examination was enough for me to be discharged temporarily with a twenty-per-cent pension—180 francs a year. I drew that pension every year until my arrest. I wonder what has happened to it since then. I am sure I had no right to anything in prison: it would be comic for a criminal to be pensioned by the State. Unless it accumulated somewhere in an office waiting for the end of my sentence. My sentence will have no end, and I bequeath my fortune as an old pensioner to whoever wants it.

It did not take long. I went to hospital and then to

barracks. My good Captain, who had already foreseen my discharge, had prepared all the documents for my release. In next to no time I had signed everything that was necessary, returned my equipment, recovered my civilian belongings (the suits were now too big for me), went to the paymaster to draw my travelling-money and made my way to the station.

I said my good-byes but without offering to pay for the traditional round of drinks. I could think of nothing but the bank and the place I should find waiting there for me. During that seven-hour journey I imagined the most terrible things—that there would be no vacancy on the staff or that they would find me too ill. But I felt no trace of my weakness nor the throbbing of my wound. Nothing at all. Had Bloch-Templier ordered me to take part in manœuvres in order to return to the Boulevard Haussmann I should have run back at the risk of a relapse. Like a dog. . . .

I arrived in the rue de l'Isly half an hour after midnight. The Palois were playing *manille* with two clients in an empty café. "This is a surprise!" they both cried, and asked me why I was so thin. They told me I was very lucky as the lodger in my old room had just left. Palois went down to the cellar and fetched up the parcel I had left in September in which I had packed all my things. An hour later I was in my old room again. How good it seemed, but I did not close an eye for thinking of the Boulevard Haussmann.

The following morning I was at the bank by nine o'clock. I ran straight into Provost in the hall. "Hullo," he said. "On leave?" and shook my hand as though there had never been any difference between us. I made my way to the staff manager's office and M. Sarrazin received me almost at once. He had changed one of his typists, but the other one winked at me and I blushed. "We did not expect you so soon," said M. Sarrazin, so I explained to him what had happened. Then he telephoned to the chief and told him of my return and the reasons for it.

The chief sent for me. From that moment I seemed to be living in a dream. Yes, I seemed to have gone back five years, when I saw the white-haired usher with his chain, the great board-room with its plants, the mannequins and lighted globes of the *Printemps*. But this time I was not sent off with a form in my hand. We walked over a thick carpet to a double door which the old man opened without a word.

M. Bloch-Templier was seated at an enormous table. He stood up and led me by the arm to one of the windows. "You must build your strength up," he said in his authoritative voice. As I stammered out a few words of thanks he said with a smile, "At least the barracks haven't changed you, I see." Then he sat down, and looking me straight in the face, went on, "So you're going into 'Financial Intelligence'?" He sent for M. Roussel, the head of the department and his right-hand man, and they discussed my future.

M. Roussel already knew me as he had lectured in one of the courses of the professional school. We went downstairs together, like comrades. His department was on the second floor in quiet, spacious offices with eight clerks in all, quite different from the ground floor. M. Roussel introduced me to his assistant, M. Fabrègues, and to each of his collaborators in turn. They were all more or less young, but all very well dressed with clean, manicured hands. I had never been into this room before, but had always imagined the occupants would be like that.

I spent two years in 'Financial Intelligence' in the Bloch-Templier bank, at the end of which both M. Roussel and his assistants considered me to be their star junior. Thanks to my little dossiers, the firm embarked upon several undertakings which brought them in millions, and rejected others which would have swallowed up as many millions. I had predicted the currency market fluctuations better than anyone else.

I'm telling you the truth, Denis, for it is not a question of blowing my own trumpet. If you remember, everybody agreed on this point. It is true they insinuated at the same time that I had tried to inspire confidence in order to facilitate my later deceit. M. Bloch-Templier used the word 'Machiavellian'. Poor man! He preferred to look like an unsuccessful psychologist and to make things worse for me rather than admit he could not understand it. And as the great chief was all for Machiavellianism you can imagine that all the others followed suit, big and small, from Roussel to Provost—yes, even Provost. Well, he was thinking of his job.

What should I have done in his place, Denis? We are all dogs when it is a question of defending our livelihood. Perhaps it is only because of my seven years and the fact that I am no longer hungry that I shall be capable of making a gesture, a real one.

How could men like M. Bloch-Templier and his general staff be so grossly mistaken about an employee they had known from childhood and whose career they had followed for ten consecutive years, apart from eight months' military service? Would a Machiavelli be capable of working for ten years for the sake of abusing the confidence of his chief and then be caught like me? Should I have returned 400,000 francs out of 650,000? And above all, should I have quitted 'Financial Intelligence', the best place in the world for speculation and growing rich in the most legal manner possible? Of course, the salary I was paid at A.P., Ltd., was an attractive one. Forty thousand francs a year for a boy of twenty-three who had started at 75 francs a month, with an increase to 50,000 after a very short time. But after the fall of the franc, large salaries did not surprise anyone, and then a Machiavelli knows how to refuse certain material advantages when he can envisage greater possibilities for the future. On the contrary, with what joy and emotion did I accept that offer! When M. Bloch-Templier offered me the job I could have kissed his hands, and he realized this, for he said to me, "You are a good lad."

I OUGHT to have asked you the other day—which day? I forget how I'm living at present. Yes, the day of my release from Melun, Thursday—I ought to have asked you on Thursday if you had followed my trial, then I should have no need to give you details which perhaps you already know. But on Thursday I had no idea I was going to write to you like this. Now it's better that I explain everything.

Well, this is how M. Bloch-Templier in his own words outlined the aims of A.P., Ltd. An American engineer named Adams, who had settled in France after the war, had invented a stabilizing gear for aeroplanes which it appears enabled machines of all types to be handled with a degree of safety hitherto unknown. After exhaustive trials a rich capitalist, M. Maudière, had, with the help of a small group, obtained a sole patent and this group was to be formed into a Company for the Exploitation of the Adams Process, the A.P., Ltd. Our bank had been approached to raise the money, but M. Bloch-Templier found the business so interesting that he decided to finance the scheme personally. He was offered the chairmanship of the board, but preferred to act as an ordinary director, for in a business like that, which required a very few men and a small staff—one had only to protect the rights each time our invention was sold and to collect the profits from the factories which constructed them—the chairman of the board could quite easily share this title with that of managing director.

M. Maudière was the obvious man for this joint position. Whenever I think of him now I only see his pale face behind the 400,000 francs I placed one day on his table. I find it difficult to see him as the man I had always known—a small, active old man with polished nails, spats, a braided morning-coat and his hair parted so perfectly that it looked as if it were a wig. In fact, a pocket-size, elderly *beau.* He looked me up and down from head to foot with that look I had come to know so well from Janson and M. Florigny. I was, however, better dressed than before my military service.

In the 'Intelligence Department' I had spent some money on new clothes; nothing very spectacular, for I always maintained that nothing suited me, that I held myself too badly and looked too clumsy. A lack of poise. My colleagues had never mentioned the fact, but I was not mistaken. I had bought a suit on the Boulevard Saint-Martin at the Royal Tailors. Provost had given me this address. His suits sat well on him, as well as on the dummies in the window, but naturally he chose them of light-coloured material. Whereas I was not bold enough, and ordered a plain black one.

I have just got up to look at myself in the mirror. It needed courage. Would you believe it, the suit I bought after leaving you on Thursday, at a ready-made outfitter's hardly superior to the Royal Tailors, is exactly like that black one I wore in 'Intelligence', just as lugubrious—even more lugubrious. For at least in those days it was offset by a young, although not particularly attractive, face. I do not think I was actually ugly. But now, my thin body and black beard, on top of this suit! Why did I choose black for both suit and overcoat? I did not choose it. I let the salesman advise me. And I followed his advice because I thought it was better. I must look like Deibler.

At that time I did not inspire fear—only mirth. I remember one day, on a visit to the staff manager's office, I heard M. Sarrazin's elder typist whisper into the new girl's ear, "Here's the little bumpkin." I, who since my return from the regiment had hoped she'd make eyes at me! I think I had even gone upstairs especially to see her, for I could just as well have telephoned M. Sarrazin instead of bothering to go and see him. Her colleague looked up and laughed too. This did not prevent things happening between the latter and myself when I was working at A.P., Ltd., and at that time Marthe would have liked to have been in her shoes.

Forgive me, I'm getting things mixed again; but this question of clothes played such an important role at that period of my life. The first time I found myself alone with M. Maudière in the still-empty offices of A.P., Ltd., in the rue d'Astorg, he said to me: "My young friend"—he always called me that until the day when, like everyone else, he apostrophized me as Machiavellian—"if M. Bloch-Templier had not assured me that you were the right man for this job, I should never have believed it. You dress in the most disastrous manner. I know it looks very intellectual, but that style is valueless in business." That style! He soon perceived that it was not affectation.

Taking advantage of my new wealth, I ordered tailor-made suits, hand-made shoes and fashionable felt hats. M. Maudière shook his head with a contemptuous grimace. He soon gave up talking to me about my clothes, but he had a way of looking at the set of my collar and fondling his own that made me want to sink through the floor. You see, in 'Financial Intelligence' this all began to count in my eyes, particularly after the day I heard myself called a bumpkin by a pretty girl, but I had other things to think about. My work obsessed me even more than before the regiment.

I remained at the bank after closing-time, took documents home with me and wrote my reports at night. Two years during which I despised all pleasure. I went to the cinema sometimes with Provost and one or two colleagues and occasionally for a little walk by myself on Sundays. But I thought of my dossiers the whole time.

At A.P., Ltd., it was all quite different. My work consisted in being on the spot. I dictated letters, interviewed people, attended board meetings and wrote up the minutes. For me, idleness. And even if I had tried to work harder I should not have been able to, for the business looked after itself, earned as much money as it needed and afforded no work except accountancy.

I often wondered what use I was, and was surprised at earning so much money with so little effort when my night work in the bank had brought me in so little. But I quickly got used to it, and at the same time began to bother about myself. It's all so difficult to explain. From one day to the next I had the impression of having joined the ranks of the powerful. Admittedly I had no vote at board meetings, but I was there. I heard all their secrets, and when various points were discussed, M. Maudière or M. Bloch-Templier sometimes asked, "Have you any suggestions, Gallon?" and occasionally I had one to make. I was offered cigarettes, and although I never liked tobacco I smoked them.

Those board meetings were more like family reunions! M. Maudière, M. Bloch-Templier and a third, M. Calbourdin of Calbour Aeroplanes–three people, the minimum laid down by law. In any case the whole Company consisted of only twelve, including the three directors, who between them had taken up the 1000 shares that made up the capital of 100,000 francs. There were no share certificates as they had not bothered to print them: the holdings merely figured in the share register under their owners' names. They call that 'allotted but not issued', you know. . . . And each of the shareholders had received a receipt from the Company in place of shares.

Should I be here now if these details had been arranged differently? Of course. I should have found some other way.

The thunder and the wind have ceased. It is very quiet. Just now I heard a car pass. I thought it might be him returning, for he is certain to have a car—I saw the garage on the Loire side. I was frightened. I thought he might have come to tell his wife that he would have to leave again immediately for three or six months. But the car passed at high speed, blowing its horn. Well, I should have waited for him: I am in no hurry. I say that, but it's a lie: I am in a hurry. I know perfectly well that if I were not writing to you, and did not feel that you were in sympathy, this waiting would be intolerable. When one should already be dead, each second of life is a torture. You see, Denis, it is not taking my life that needs courage, but waiting.

I shall soon have to speak of him. I am hurrying or pretending to hurry, but in actual fact am I not trying to postpone that moment? However, it is vital for me to explain. It won't take long. A.P., Ltd., was founded in June 1925, and I had just been to my second tribunal and been discharged for good. I admit that I made my preparations seriously and did everything one can do in such a case. The only time in my life I was deliberately Machiavellian. But I could not see myself returning to barracks just at the moment when I had been offered such a good post. My little subterfuges had succeeded quite well the previous year, and besides, the sight of my scar impressed the doctors favourably, and I still suffered from adhesions. It needed prison to make me feel them no more.

During the two years between the foundation of A.P., Ltd., and my holidays in Vichy, where everything began, I tried to become worthy of my new surroundings. A man of the world. . . . No, I would not wear spats like M. Maudière or make an appointment with the manicurist each week; or rather I wanted to arrive at the point where I could wear spats and be manicured without looking ridiculous, do you understand? Poise.

M. Bloch-Templier consulted me occasionally at board meetings, and on the day of the general meeting invited me to lunch with some of the shareholders, but I still felt the gulf between all those people and myself. They spoke of parties, hunting, marriageable daughters and children with brilliant school records.

I must tell you that I noticed the vulgarity in some of them like Calbour. Success alone had given them something which made me servile. I wondered, now that I too was rich—for by comparison I was very well off as a bachelor with no responsibilities—why at the same time I had not gained their self-assurance.

But as opposed to these vulgarians, some of them were extremely cultured, like M. Maudière, Bloch-Templier and others. I remember a conversation between M. Maudière and one of our shareholders, M. Vital, on tetralogy which astounded me. That day I told myself that I needed a background and that fine manners result from cultivating the mind. Idiotic, wasn't it? But it doesn't matter. Naturally, since I had left the army I had given up my manual of philosophy and I never looked at it again.

I joined a library and read novels and periodicals. I came across your name several times, but you were mainly interested in social questions and politics, and I would have nothing to do with those subjects because they reminded me of Maman. I was envious, however, of your notoriety after *The Tragedy of Bienvenu Gasmere*. I remembered that although you and Fournier had won first prize jointly in French in the Sixth, I had been second. At that moment I began to write a 'society' novel. I had enough sense to tear it all up after twenty pages. I studied the classics, went to the Comédie-Française and the Odéon.

I read books on art, historical studies, visited the Louvre and the Carnavalet, the Invalides, the Sainte-Chapelle and everything else. One day I even took a seat in a charabanc in the rue de Hanovre—'Paris by night'. A guide gave explanations, but in English. I did not understand very much and had forgotten my English since Janson, so to learn it again I took a year's course at a Berlitz school.

I went to concerts, to the opera, the Opéra-Comique and to cafés where good orchestras played. What a revelation! Not difficult or modern music, but *Faust*, *Tannhäuser*, *Carmen*, *La Tosca*, and Beethoven, Saint-Saëns and Massenet. I hummed the tunes to myself on my way home. My eyes were full of tears and my heart beat wildly.

You have no idea how much I desired a friend at that time. I felt that music must be listened to in company. I went out occasionally with Provost, but he had become engaged, so I decided that a feminine companion would be even better than a friend. I should have liked a fiancée too, but unfortunately they don't grow on trees.

One evening M. Bloch-Templier, who had some papers to give me for the Company, took me in his car from A.P., Ltd., to the Boulevard Haussmann—in that great black Rolls around which I used to hover when I was a junior clerk working in the 'portfolio'.

It was just after six o'clock, the time the staff was leaving. We got out of the car in the rue Auber, and who should we run into but M. Sarrazin's two typists, Marthe and the other. M. Bloch-Templier, who was in front, went straight on into the building; but I took off my hat with a great gesture, and they answered my greeting with an air of such stupefaction that I laughed to myself for a long time afterwards.

When I left the bank a quarter of an hour later they were still on the pavement. Marthe told me that they were delighted to see me again, that they knew of my new post and everything. She suggested that I should take them somewhere for an *apéritif*.

I took them to the Café de la Paix just to show them what had happened to the country bumpkin. Marthe never stopped talking, using all sorts of little mannerisms which irritated me immensely. I had not forgiven her insult. Her friend Alice did not open her mouth, but looked at me in the most touching manner.

When they got up to go, Marthe gave me her address and told me to get in touch with her whenever I liked. I plucked up the courage to ask Alice where she lived. Marthe gave me a venomous look, but Alice blushed and told me all the same.

On the following day I sent her a little note inviting her to the cinema on the following Saturday. I held her hand during the picture, and as we left she leant heavily on my arm. I could not take her home–I had moved from rue de l'Isly in favour of a very respectable hotel in the rue Caumartin where I should never have dared to take a woman, particularly after midnight. So we chose the first little hotel we saw, and she was very sweet and simple and at the same time loving. So was I.

This was the first time in my life I had ever experienced anything that resembled love. We did not stay long, for she had to return home, and then for Alice once a thing was done it was all over. She was only allowed out on Saturday nights, and had to stay at home on other days. I told her that I should like to know her family better, which was my way of saying that I was serious. She could not have understood me, for she burst out laughing and said, "What an idea!" This was a great disappointment,

One evening I took her to the Opéra-Comique. She had accepted with pleasure, but told me later that she preferred the cinema, or better still, fairs and circuses. After an affair that lasted a month and a half she failed to turn up at our usual rendezvous without a word of explanation. I was rather sad, not because of her but because of love. It had to be like that, I thought, but I also believed that love would come later with everything else, and that I was merely not ready for it. I did not even feel a wish to go to the bank and see if anything had happened to her.

Poor Alice! They forced her to appear at the trial—obviously a trick of Marthe's. How the poor girl wept! She kept on repeating, "If only I had known, if only I had known!" In my defence they sullied her reputation, she who was no better or worse than anyone else. Justice is a fine thing. What, may I ask, was her testimony worth? Nothing. They could not even represent me as a Don Juan! That was my lawyer's theme: *cherchez la femme!* He wasn't so far wrong, after all. I remember his attitude. He turned to me brusquely, as much as to say: "Is that your secret? Now will you speak?" And I, obsessed by an image, thought, If you could only see what I see.

The episode with Alice happened in 1926, just before the holidays. Three weeks of holidays during which I wandered round Paris—Versailles, Fontainebleau, Chartres. When they came to an end, however, I realized how foolish I had been. I should have employed them differently by going to the seaside or to a spa, one of the places where my employers went—the only possible places to meet the society I dreamed of and to profit by it. For there no one would know my origin and I should not be a marked man as in Paris.

I wish I could remember the moment when this idea came into my head, that moment which destroyed a whole life. I can't remember. In any case, that split second was no more responsible than the one in which I accepted the job in A.P., Ltd., or the one when I issued from my mother's womb. Two deaths to atone for that is really not too much.

My idea of going to the sea or to a spa preoccupied me the whole winter and I determined to carry out my plan next year without fail. One day I, who had wanted so much to see the sea again, chose a spa. I have no idea why. Perhaps a poster, 'Spend the Season at Vichy'. Those two words, 'Season' and 'Vichy', side by side on a Morris column in the Boulevard des Capucines on the corner of the rue Daunou.

It was spring and beautiful weather. 'Spend the Season at Vichy.' Wonderful words, a gala each day and even pageants. And the Casino des Fleurs and the races, the golf, the pigeon-shooting and the regattas. Was it really like that, or have my memories become all jumbled? Oh, it's going to be so difficult, Denis. I have to be so lucid to tell you everything so calmly, with every detail, while it is precisely that which has always kept my lips sealed.

Excuse this blot. It seems as though even my pen is unwilling. Why, why? Can a prospective corpse feel a trace of self-respect—of self-respect or despair?

Perhaps writing has made me tired. What time is it? I should love to hear the simple ticking of a clock. This silence is terrifying. Or the wind. Yes, I should even prefer the wind to spring up again. Everything is so still. I should like to see the inkpot move or the shutters open of their own accord. Now I am beginning to breathe with difficulty, as last night. From fear? That would be stupid. It must be the cold. . . . It must be three or four o'clock in the morning, and the air always becomes chilly at that hour. I am going to bed, to sleep until breakfast-time. I must sleep.

(*The following morning. Sunday.*)

I HAVE just come back, my face and hands soaking wet. This morning when I heard it raining I needed a lot of will-power not to rush out immediately. And as it happened, the chambermaid came later than usual. It's Sunday. But as soon as I had swallowed my coffee I dressed without even washing and ran down to the river. Rain, Denis, pouring rain! I took off my hat to feel it better on my face, in my ears and on my neck. I should have liked to tear off this beard and moustache which prevented it from washing me. I held out my hands to it and would have liked to thank it. However, I had to put my hat on again because people were coming out of their houses with umbrellas on their way to Mass. The bells were ringing very loudly. I did not want to mar the assembly at the church. But I was a stranger and people looked at me as they passed.

The hotel proprietor must have spoken about me, for in the tobacconist's where I bought a paper and another pen the shopkeeper said to me, "So you work on Sundays too?" and I replied, "The same as you." He laughed heartily. He will remember this joke later on.

The rain did not last long enough. Suddenly the sun

came out, and it was so fine and the air so sweet that I went back to the hotel. The door of my room was open, with a bucket and broom on the threshold. The maid was just finishing her cleaning, and singing as she worked. She too will have known me and spoken to me. Perhaps she will be the first to arrive after the shot. No, she would be too frightened. It will be the hotel keeper. Not yet, though—no news from opposite. But that does not surprise me, for I was told that he would not return until the beginning of the week.

Just as I approached the hotel I met all of them—the mother and her two children, the lady in the light dress and the woman in black, each one carrying a missal. At this very moment, perhaps, they are praying for him. They should not be praying to heaven, but to me. But even if you were to kneel at my feet—you and the children—you would get no mercy from me, my fine ladies. That would be too easy.

What does it mean when a revolver jams? I have often read in the newspapers: 'The gun did not go off. It jammed.'

He comes towards me out of the house. I open the window wide. I aim and fire, and the shot does not go off. . . . Impossible. That can happen only with old, neglected revolvers, badly oiled. Should one oil a revolver? If I dared to lock myself in I would take a look at mine, but I dare not. At night I can slip it under my bolster without looking at it. In any case it would be quite likely to go off in my face as it is already loaded with the safety catch removed. Thank you very much. That would be premature.

I ought to have asked more information of the armourer. When he suggested I should try it I refused, for I thought he would see at once that I didn't know how to use it and would wonder, 'Why is he buying a revolver'? I behaved like an idiot. One also reads sometimes, 'Pointing the weapon at himself, the assassin tried to take justice into his own hands, but the weapon jammed.' He dead and I alive? Not for very long, anyhow. A murder is not like a swindle, and one day in the early morning . . . For they will call it a murder. But to achieve my end I should have to go through another interrogation, another trial and then prison again. No, I do not deserve this new delay.

"A first-class job," the armourer said to me. "It is the most expensive we have in the shop." My cleaning-up operation will be finished. What a state all these good people will be in next Sunday when they go to Mass! And you perhaps will already have read these pages.

I suddenly thought that the police might find them here and confiscate them, so I must dispatch them to you as quickly as possible. And then, supposing one of the post-office officials, intrigued by my presence in this hole, should take it upon himself to open the package and learn of the deed before I have accomplished it? That must never happen. It is better that they fall into the hands of the police once it is over.

As I have begun I shan't stop now. Will this prevent me from writing to you as sincerely as before? Certainly not. I don't care a — for the police. They can read to their hearts' content when I'm dead and they won't understand a thing; and then so much the better if something forces me to control myself, to be lucid.

The day I risked telling M. Maudière of my holiday plans he looked at me with curiosity and murmured, "Not at all a bad idea," and immediately gave me a few tips. If I took his advice I should take a room at the Hôtel Imperator overlooking the park. It was not the most luxurious palace in Vichy, but it was a good hotel and I could mention his name to the manager, who was a very obliging fellow.

I wrote immediately on A.P., Ltd., notepaper, the managing director's paper. To think that I could just as well have used plain notepaper! I received a reply by return of post. A fine room with running water and three meals *en pension.* Ninety francs a day plus taxes and service, making a hundred-odd francs in all. It would cost me about two thousand francs for three weeks, not very much considering what I had saved out of my salary and my share of the profits. For the success of this business had exceeded by far the most optimistic expectations. Not very much, and yet . . . A hundred francs a day for the Gallon boy, 'the kid with the pinafore', 'the criminal', 'the convict'. Perhaps I might meet Palaiseau or Bruneval or Mme de Bimont.

The manager asked me to tell M. Maudière that the Grand Prix de Vichy would be particularly brilliant that year, and closed his letter by assuring me of his special attention. There are words that become so comical when one remembers them. When I passed on this communication to my president, he replied: "Pity I can't leave Paris in August. I should have liked to see you there." I was heartily thankful that he couldn't.

I prepared my wardrobe carefully. A dinner-jacket made to measure–my first dinner-jacket–and everything to go with it; a travelling-coat, two pairs of grey flannel trousers, white shoes, etc., together with a camera and binoculars, all in a magnificent pigskin suitcase with my initials.

I left in the afternoon on Saturday the 23rd of July, travelling first class with newspapers and a book. I arrived at Vichy just before dinner. The Imperator bus was waiting at the station for me and three other guests, *habitués.*

The manager greeted me at the entrance to the hotel. He was a small, thin man with an obsequious air. He showed me personally to my room on the third floor and told me that he had a surprise for me. For the same price he had given me a room with a bath. With a great deal of beating about the bush, the manager, Chinchard, declared that he was delighted to be of service to any friend of M. Maudière.

The first time in my life that I had a bathroom to myself. And the room! Immense, with a large gleaming copper bed, fine polished furniture, carpets, lamps with pink shades and three bells for service set in the wall. Luxury, eh? When I look at my room today, the torn paper screen hiding the basin, the fireplace without a mirror and the dressing-table mirror with yellow streaks. . . . Oh, it's quite good enough for No. 9425—but there I go again!

The porter brought up my trunks and a chambermaid came to lay out my clothes. The waiter brought me the menu for dinner, *table d'hôte* and *à la carte*. I chose the latter, and even told him that I was very hungry and gave him a knowing wink.

I went out on to my balcony. It looked out over the trees of the park, but the foliage was so thick that I could not see very much except a little of the casino verandah. Below me the roof of the covered gallery hid the passers-by, but I could hear their feet on the asphalt—an extraordinary noise, which I can still hear, like rain. And then music in the distance, and the trot of victorias and the cries of the newspaper boys. It was magnificent. I lay down on my bed and looked up at the ceiling, listening with beating heart. Then dinner. But you know these luxury hotels with little lights on the tables, food served to you on silver dishes as though you were the most important person in the room.

Then I went out. My heart was still beating fast. I discovered that there were towns designed entirely to amuse women and gratify their desires. Of course, they come to Vichy primarily for their health; but that did not prevent there being brilliantly lighted shops, luxury goods, jewels, knick-knacks, lingerie, furs . . . with names that I recognized, for most of them were branches of Paris houses. But in Paris I passed by without noticing, even in the rue de la Paix, because in Paris in addition to the rue de la Paix there are also the rue d l'Annonciation, the shaby grocery that furnishes the rue de Passy, and the street of Mother Mourgues, whereas there I believe there is nothing except shops for the rich and hotels and cafés with music, all of which I discovered that first evening as in a dream. I felt good and full of admiration.

I remember saying to myself: When I am married and have children I shall return here with them, and then Maman will give way and understand. We shall go and find her and bring her here. The reason she is so terrible is because she does not know such a life exists. I was forgetting that she knew it only too well and had been employed in it.

Never mind. I met people going to the casino, the men in tails and the women in evening dress, just as in a society film. They went on foot, and this seemed quite natural on such a fine night. After an hour my head was so feverish that I went back to my hotel, thinking: Me—André Gallon—and three weeks of this life!

André Gallon. It was at Vichy that I saw my name in print for the first time. Oh, I forgot the prize lists of our youth at Janson; but as all of you—the good pupils—were also on it and I did not head the list, it slipped my memory. And then how can I admit it to you? To see my name in the prize lists was a foregone conclusion. I knew perfectly well that I should have a second in maths or in French, then . . . Whereas at Vichy!

One morning they brought up on my breakfast-tray a kind of newspaper, a large brochure, the official list of visitors with big red letters on the cover and a photograph of the Hotel de Ville. And in the second column of the first page, beneath the heading 'Hôtel Imperator', *Gallon,*

André, Paris. Why first on the list, for it was not in alphabetical order? Because I was the first arrival in the hotel since the preceding number, or because they wished to continue to show me special respect? André Gallon, Paris; André Gallon, Melun; André Gallon, nowhere. . . . This happened on Thursday the 29th. I have good reason to remember that day because on that day I met them for the first time.

During the four preceding days I had forgotten all my plans, forgotten that I had come to Vichy to learn how to live. I relaxed like a lizard in the sun. It never entered my head to visit the casino or to go on an excursion. I was content to read the playbills or watch the cars full of English leave every morning for the Chaise-Dieu, the Puy de Dôme or the grand tour of the Auvergne. I lingered by the springs, watching the invalids drinking and breathing that strange odour of hot sulphur water. I took coffee in La Restauration to listen to a Roumanian orchestra playing waltzes.

On Thursday, that Thursday I had seen my name in the lists, I was sitting about midday in one of those armchairs which the park hotels place along their fronts on the pavement. My eyes followed the cars and the pedestrians but without really seeing them. I said to myself that I must get to know people if I wanted to profit by my stay, and at that minute, that very minute, they came out of the park, crossed the street and sat down on my right. There was only one empty chair between him and myself. He stared at me so insistently that I could not help casting an eye in his direction. At last he remarked: "What magnificent weather, isn't it?"

"Absolutely magnificent," I replied.

"You're a Parisian, I'm sure," he went on.

"Yes, I am."

He turned heavily towards the young girl at his side. "Like us," he said. "Like us."

Until then I had seen only her profile. She leaned a little forward with a faint smile but seemed completely disinterested in our conversation. As though to excuse her he introduced me with a florid gesture. "My daughter," he said, and added, "My name is Dhuibert, Pascal Dhuibert, industrialist." That is how things began, Denis. I did not think they would be so easy to relate. "And you," he asked, "are M. Gallon if I'm not mistaken. I heard Chinchard mention your name." Thereupon he began to talk of Vichy, which he had visited for years for the cure. "This is the first time I've brought her with me," he said, pointing to his daughter. "It makes it much more amusing." We both laughed.

I could not take my eyes off that profile, so innocent and different from the man's. Dhuibert had a fat face with a big nose and a large dark drooping moustache which hid his mouth and emphasized his double chin. Rather like the head of a butcher, and even more so as he was wearing a cap—admittedly a very smart one. A head which suited his frame. But his eyes—they struck me from the very start—little bright black eyes between slitted eyelids that seemed unwilling to open, and so wide that they nearly reached to his temples. He looked as if he were examining you through his eyelashes, as if he were weighing you up and could read your very thoughts.

He was obviously aware of the impression he gave, for he often looked away to relax his neck and he stretched his legs out as my father used to do.

I wanted to say to the girl: "When my father sat down he stretched out his legs just as yours does," but she remained motionless and if I had dared I should have moved my chair to see her better. According to Dhuibert's movements I could see her profile, her neck with an enormous chignon set very low on the nape. Once she patted this bun with her left hand and adjusted a hairpin which had slipped out of place. I felt a shiver run through my whole body.

Suddenly Dhuibert got up and said: "Half past twelve already. Time for lunch." The girl got up too, gave me a little nod and went into the hotel, completely hidden by Dhuibert's silhouette. I waited a little before going in too.

While I was eating I looked round the room to see if I could see them, but the dining-room was in two parts and apparently they were eating in the other. Supposing they don't want to push our acquaintance further, I thought. Supposing they found me too dull. I shall greet them when we meet but I shall never have the courage to speak to them first.

Two hours later I found myself with Dhuibert in a large open car with Paule sitting between us. They had invited me in the hall after lunch and we went for tea to the Ardoisière, a delicious spot beneath the pines at the edge of a torrent. Thus in a few hours my plans had materialized to an extent I should never have believed possible. I had been chosen, I, as an acquaintance by an important man and his daughter, the most beautiful creature in the world.

Already during the afternoon she had become much more amiable. She spoke to me in the car and asked me the name of a tree, which I was unable to tell her. A little farther on she made me listen to the song of a bird while Dhuibert spoke in his loud voice to the chauffeur. He questioned him about certain of the big landed proprietors (it was a hired car) and seemed to know all of them. He knew that Mr. X had made millions by speculating in mining shares and that M. de Y had a son who had just messed up a fine marriage. I remember that I pricked up my ears at the word marriage. I wondered what intention Dhuibert had for his daughter or if she were not already engaged to one of those young rich men's sons who had always made me so unhappy, like Jean Raphaël-Ambert, for example. I suffered. Yes, as quickly as that. It was love at first sight.

At tea-time I was sitting opposite her and did not know where to look. At her face?—my insistence might have displeased her; at her hands?—with the bright polished nails, she would have noticed that I was following all her gestures; at her legs?—her dress was so short that her knees could be seen. . . .

The other day when I came out of Melun and crossed the town with my suitcase on the way to the station I noticed—and yet I hardly ever thought of such things I assure you—that women no longer show their legs. I even said to myself, Only fifty kilometres from Paris and they're not smart any more. I did not understand until I had arrived at the Gare de Lyon: fashions change in seven years.

How can I, who am forcing myself to tell you things in their right order without exaggerating and without adding anything to my thoughts, interrupt my narrative to tell you something so stupid? But there you are, once more things seem so difficult to explain.

We saw each other every day, and during the hours when I remained alone, I waited. And at night when I returned to my room very late, for with them I had to visit the casino, I could not sleep. Dhuibert had naturally guessed. Every time I joined them in the hall he cried, loud enough for me to hear, "Paule, here is your devoted escort," and he would laugh with his terrible little eyes and smack me on the back. Paule looked rather embarrassed and said, "You mustn't pay any attention to his teasing, M. Gallon." One day I summoned up enough courage to reply, "But your father is quite right, mademoiselle, you know very well that . . ." I could not finish the phrase. She laughed in turn and Dhuibert replied, "Isn't he sweet?"

Talking about the casino, on our return from l'Ardoisière the first day Dhuibert asked me if I went there often. They went almost every evening. Paule liked the theatre and music and quite enjoyed gambling. I rushed immediately to get a permanent card, and as on the following night they were giving a grand gala performance with Chaliapin in Don Quixote I booked three tickets, as I wished to show Dhuibert that I knew how to live and to return his hospitality.

The following evening, in my new dinner-jacket, I went into the casino with them. Everybody looked at Paule, who was most elegantly dressed. I cannot explain to you, but she was resplendent. Her jewels must have cost a fortune—a diamond bracelet as wide as two fingers, an enormous solitaire on her left hand and two in her ears. Her dark hair was parted in the centre and seemed to be cut in two halves when one saw her full face. Men stopped and stared. Some smiled and others looked with such desire that I felt inclined to hit them, and yet at the same time I was glowing with pride.

Walking slowly between Dhuibert and myself, with her lips parted and looking radiantly happy, she seemed to notice nothing. There was no trace left of the cold, indifferent girl of the day before. Her red lips showed up the whiteness of her teeth, and were so well made up they looked like a heart.

Once in the concert hall—that large gilded hall full of elegant people—I suddenly felt quite alone. The day before in the car I imagined that I had attained my goal: now, while we were listening to Chaliapin, I was already thinking about the end of my holidays, of Maudière, A.P., Ltd., and the hotel in the rue Caumartin. Besides, Dhuibert was wearing tails. And to think that I had allowed my tailor to persuade me when choosing between the two that a dinner-jacket was better! This was how I tortured my mind, but I did also listen to the music, breathed in Paule's perfume and refrained from touching her bare arm, which she might have regarded as disrespectful.

In the interval we went into the gambling room—another discovery for me. I noticed that both Dhuibert and Paule enjoyed it. I risked a ten-franc piece and asked Paule to stake for me. "Five is always my lucky number," she said. I tried it and the ball came to rest in five and the croupier's rake pushed a handful of counters towards me. The people standing by must have heard Paule's remark and looked at us. She picked up the counters, called the changer and said: "That's too good. You mustn't lose them." In any case the warning bell had gone for the second act of the opera.

But Dhuibert and she both preferred the races, and naturally they took me with them each Sunday. Each Sunday. There were only three. But those three weeks—actually only eighteen days as I had not met them until after my arrival—seemed to have lasted a year. And yet how short I found them while I was living them! As soon as I woke up I looked at my watch and was sorry to see the second hand pass so slowly. They came down late and I followed suit and stayed in bed day-dreaming. For the moment that would soon come was the highlight of the day for me.

Between twelve and half past Paule and I went for a walk alone in the new park. Dhuibert pretended that this little walk before lunch tired him. He was taking the cure, but this did not prevent his drinking vintage wines and paying no attention to the diet, and he preferred to sit outside the hotel reading the papers. He dismissed us with a: "Run along, you young people. When you get to my age . . ." He laughed and we waved to him as we turned the corner.

The Allier was only two steps away. We walked slowly along the bank beneath the magnificent trees and past the flowers. I photographed Paule feeding the two ibises on the little pond or with the duck and its ducklings. She had a way of bursting out laughing that made people turn round, and quite disconcerted me.

Admittedly we did not speak very much and she often seemed to be thinking of something else, until one day I had the courage to say to her: "You are bored with me, mademoiselle. There must surely be other men whom you would find more amusing." She seemed to wrench herself out of a dream and replied: "Of course not. What an idea!" She laid her hand on my arm for a brief second, which thrilled me with happiness. That same day over coffee I found myself alone with Dhuibert—we now ate together.

After lunch Paule had gone upstairs to lie down and Dhuibert and I were talking. He said to me: "You are a serious man, aren't you, Gallon? I suppose I can trust you. The fact is, Paule is very attached to you. I can see it. I would not like that child . . . You understand me? At first sight you would think she was sophisticated like all the modern young girls, but she is the most ingenuous creature in the world. So I beg of you, no over-frivolous conversations, a little tact and delicacy. I speak to you as a friend. Don't think for one minute that I'm interfering with your courtship. The man who can touch the heart of my daughter. . . . Well, I'm not one to gainsay my children."

Yes, Dhuibert said all that to me. He seemed happy to get it off his chest and his words intoxicated him, but I assure you they intoxicated me even more. Paule was attached to me? I was amazed and stupefied. Dhuibert noticed this, for his little eyes began to twinkle and he said, "Tell me, can you see yourself one day becoming my son-in-law?" but he added: "We mustn't go too fast—and above all no jokes upon this subject in front of my daughter! Anyhow it's not as simple as all that. We haven't known each other very long, and people don't marry like that. Paule has a great many needs and I have thoroughly spoiled her. Should you have any intentions you must grow up first and then we'll see. In any case you have made a very good start."

From the very beginning of our acquaintance he had shown a great interest in my activities. I told him that I was in A.P., Ltd. He knew a great deal about the company and said that he had even tried to buy some shares and asked me to give him the tip before anyone else if any of our shareholders wanted to sell. "I'll take any there are on offer, and at no matter what price." He seemed surprised and a little disappointed when I told him that I was secretary to the board. "I don't know why," he admitted, "but I had an idea you were the managing director." But as soon as I described to him the importance of my position and the confidence they had in me—I was frightened of being once more rejected and despised—Dhuibert declared that they must consider me to have very exceptional abilities to have entrusted me with such a job.

This conversation took place in front of Paule, who showed no trace of absentmindedness that day and was all ears as if she were delighted to discover I was not a nonentity.

Dhuibert exchanged confidences with me. The thing that interested him most was to create, to put an affair on its feet and to get it going. As soon as it gave a maximum return he went on to something else, retaining, naturally, an interest in the old one—not always, because, like every man who refuses to compromise, he had many enemies and sometimes these enemies got the better of him. He quoted several important businesses which he had founded on his own and from which he had had to retire as a result of amalgamations designed to cut him out. Actually I knew several of these businesses that he mentioned from having studied them at Bloch-Templier's, but I had never come across the name of Pascal Dhuibert. But how could I have disbelieved him, as there appeared no doubt as to his credentials?

Either that day or the one following, Chinchard, the hotel manager, spoke to me about him. Since my arrival the little man had always greeted me as I passed and made some remark about the weather or asked me if I were enjoying myself at Vichy. He was much more familiar with Dhuibert, although he never lost his obsequious manner, but I caught them several times laughing together or speaking in undertones or reading letters. When I approached they separated immediately and Dhuibert cried, "*Au revoir*, my friend," or "That's understood, *mon vieux*," and Chinchard would bow.

That day, instead of confining himself to some polite remark from a distance as I passed, he came up to me in the hall, which was empty except for the porter behind his desk and the lift boy at the far end of the hall. Chinchard told me that he was happy to have been to a certain extent instrumental in bringing about my friendship with M. Dhuibert, that exceptional man, that astonishing live wire to whom so many people owed their fortune, etc., etc. It was he who had told Dhuibert I was staying in the hotel. He even apologized for having thought I was managing director of A.P., Ltd., and for having mentioned me in that capacity. He had surmised as much from my letter-heading when I had written in July.

Suddenly I understood how close the relationship was between Dhuibert and Chinchard, and also that the former must have scolded him for his false information. But I attached no importance to it. I merely thought that I was being well looked after at the Imperator. I could never have hoped for as much, and what could I say on the day

Dhuibert had alluded to Paule's attachment to me? Perhaps it was love. . . . Love?

I suddenly felt faint. It must be this tension, this effort to control myself when I think of these follies. And then as I raised my eyes I saw through my yellow curtain the house that is waiting for him and the sun on the flowers. It was too much. . . .

(*After Lunch.*)

I HAD to go down to lunch. I lunched, but not alone. I lunched with my image. An image as clear as it was at Melun. Although the dining-room was crowded today I saw only *that*. No, I must not tell you yet. I drank two cups of coffee and a brandy in a large glass. My first brandy for eight years. And do you know what happened? I saw my image and wanted to laugh. I had come up quickly to my room because I should have burst out laughing in the dining-room. I have just enjoyed my joke to the full with tears running down my beard. It's all over now . . . until the moment when I shall laugh with the joker. And it won't be alone either . . . it won't be alone.

I must go on, and if I can't control myself I will go back and have another drink. How simple it was! I was stupid not to have thought of it sooner.

. . .

From the moment I told myself that I could not be a matter of complete indifference to Paule I lived in a state of extraordinary exaltation. I had only to grow up, and that now seemed so easy. One day I told Dhuibert my life story—concealing the fact that my mother had been and might still be a charwoman—and he admired my rise; and for the first time I found it magnificent. I had only to continue. . . . A delirious joy, do you understand? And one that I naturally hid. Paule did not change very much.

Sometimes I wondered whether Dhuibert was right. She certainly guessed my anxiety, for she immediately became sweeter—a smile, a little word, a trifle, but since she seemed to be so reserved by nature these trifles I considered as weighty proofs of her feelings for me. Those days. . . . The three of us were inseparable. Motor drives every afternoon and sometimes for the whole day. On our return we would stop at a café—the Alhambra—where there were palm trees in pots and Moorish arcades, and Dhuibert would talk about his journeys and the businesses he had started in Spain or Morocco.

In the car I felt Paule against me; in the café I sat opposite them to have a better view of her. She listened to Dhuibert and I saw her profile, but from time to time she would look at me as if to draw me into the conversation. And now at the casino I was no longer afraid of touching her arm, and she did not seem to fear or resent this either. Monday was concert evening. The chandeliers were not dimmed; the hall remained lit up and this annoyed me. I felt that for music one needed even more darkness than in a theatre, and then in the darkness I might perhaps have dared to take her hand and speak of Wagner or of Beethoven. I did attempt to do this once in spite of the lights. She did not appear to notice. She turned her head often to right and left looking at the people in the boxes or paying attention to some detail of her toilette. I was bursting with the desire to say once more, "I love you."

For I had already told her this the day before at the races. It was the Sunday of the Grand Prix, our last Sunday but one. Eight days later I had to return to Paris and my work. We had not yet spoken about our separation. Dhuibert's cure would be finished shortly after my holiday, but I did not know if they intended to go on somewhere else or to return to Paris. Suddenly between two races while we were walking in the shade beneath the trees in the enclosure my heart seemed to overflow.

Dhuibert had gone to place his bets and we were alone. Paule, dressed in white and more beautiful than ever, stood out among this extremely elegant crowd. I wanted to ask her when we should meet in Paris and I said instead, "I love you."

She looked at me with some surprise with half-closed eyes. Then she laughed and placed the handle of her sunshade on my lips. I kissed the handle. There was a sweet odour of moist grass freshly watered and flowers everywhere, and flags. . . . Dhuibert returned and I was afraid he would notice my emotion, but he was thinking of the previous race in which he had backed a winner and of the next one, the Grand Prix, where he hoped to win again. I can still hear him saying, "I've put two *louis* on number three." I even remember the name of the horse—Juveilin. Paule interrupted, "Why not number five?" and Dhuibert replied: "My child, I say nothing about *la boule*. There you can do as you like, but you mustn't confuse it with racing!"

He looked at me searchingly, and I thought he could read my mind, but he turned his head away and went on: "The crowd is not so mixed here as in town. Look, there's old Rothschild over there. His Donogoo hasn't a chance, the race isn't long enough. A fine man, old Rothschild. If we had time I'd go and say good day to him." I heard all that but I still felt on my lips the pressure of the sunshade. Paule listened to Dhuibert and seemed to be interested in what he was saying.

After the races were over, in the car that took us back to Vichy I put my arm round her shoulders respectfully, hardly touching her. She did not lean against my arm but smiled. In the hall of the hotel, before we went up to our rooms, she took from her lapel the pink card on which was printed 'Enclosure—lady or child. Valid for one day' and gave it to me.

During the whole of the last week I thought of nothing but kissing her—not on the lips, no, only on the cheek or in the corner of her eye. I did not find the opportunity. I did not know how to. I did not even dare to repeat that I loved her. Besides, she did not give me very much help. We were never alone except in the park by the Allier and I couldn't very well take her arm in public. Never mind, I was happy.

The more my holidays neared their end the more affectionate she became. One day I said to her, "You mustn't be too nice, Paule"—Dhuibert had given permission for me to use her first name—"otherwise how do you expect me to forget you?" You see, I had learned to banter like a man of the world. "But I don't want you to," she replied with a laugh. "Why should you forget me? It would not be right. Or then I should have to forget you too." Words like that. . . . I repeated them constantly and they prevented me from sleeping, and I learned what it is to have sleepless nights from happiness.

On Sunday, the 14th, they both came to see me off at the station. I had chosen the last train of the day in order to postpone our separation as long as possible. So long as

I arrived in my office on Monday morning at nine o'clock . . . Dhuibert had taken us to dine on the other bank of the Allier at the pretty Château de Charmeil, which had been turned into an hotel.

We dined out on the terrace below a little hill and some trees which grew more and more indistinct as night fell. Crayfish, a chicken in burgundy–since I had known them I had almost got used to that type of menu, and I knew how to appreciate it. But that evening I had no appetite.

During the meal Dhuibert shook me out of myself. "Is it because you don't intend to see us any more that you're making that gloomy face? You're preparing an unpleasant surprise for us, are you? We shall return to Paris and not find our friend Gallon there, our friend André." I had wanted to hear that phrase so much and it moved me almost to tears.

You can imagine how I protested. I should have liked to open my heart and show my emotion, but they understood all right. I could see on their faces a satisfaction which touched me perhaps more than words.

Anyway, before the train left we arranged to meet. Dhuibert intended to spend a fortnight in the Auvergne on business and Paule would naturally accompany him, but at the beginning of September and perhaps even at the end of August they would be returning to Paris and would let me know at once. "Write and let me know the time you arrive," I said to them, "and I will return your hospitality of this evening." Dhuibert said, "We shall do that." He shook me warmly by the hand and I kissed Paule's for as long as I dared. And then, "Take your seats, please!", the green light waving, the blow of the whistle and handkerchiefs being waved. And then nothing, only the darkness and a heart beating, beating, beating.

And so that's how one falls in love. And for some people it turns out quite successful. Incredible!

The moment I set foot in A.P., Ltd., I was received by a chorus of exclamations from the chief accountant, from Mme Corcelles, my typist, and everyone else. "How brown you are!" "You do look well!" "Holidays seem to suit you. . . ." I felt very happy and smiled in my mind at Paule.

When M. Maudière appeared he looked me up and down and murmured: "My young friend, you look as if you've come into a legacy. You have the look of a bright young man who just buried his mother-in-law. Unless"—he gave me a wink—"you're thinking of adopting one?"

He said this so pleasantly that I felt almost inclined to let him into my secret. I should have liked so much to talk about Paule. At the same time it would have offset everything that subconsciously shocked me in his jest about a future mother-in-law.

Dhuibert had told me one day when we were alone of the great sorrow of his life. Two days after giving birth to Paule . . . "An admirable creature, ten times more beautiful than her daughter, I assure you." He took out his pocketbook and put his large hairy hand on it saying: "Her photo's inside there. It never leaves me." Then he put it back in his pocket, and added in an undertone: "Don't ever mention this to my daughter. The poor angel has never got over having no mother."

But M. Maudière did not wait for my reply. He began to talk about his own health, and of the holidays he would not be taking for reasons he never told me. And all the while he grumbled and took out from a filing cabinet a bundle of current dossiers.

The opportunity had passed and never recurred. M. Maudière continued to treat me as he had done before my holidays. When I think of it today I feel I could not have changed as much as I thought. However, his expression 'a bright young man' . . . It is to be supposed that M. Maudière found it easier to keep his old opinion of me and I really could not have cared less. Yes, I am sure that after my return from Vichy and up to the beginning of the following year I could have met no matter who–the highest in the land or even my persecutors from Janson–so long as I pleased Paule and her father I had no reason to fear anybody.

I saw myself entertaining M. Bloch-Templier, Jean Raphaël-Ambert or our board of A.P., Ltd., who were the highest one could meet in the world of finance. They would be bound to cluster round the beautiful Madame André Gallon. They might even try to flirt with her. But Paule would not allow this, obviously, and I should not only be respected but even envied. . . .

During the following weeks I received several postcards from Royat, Clermont-Ferrand, then from Carcassonne and Toulouse. Only a few lines on the weather or about the monument which the card represented–nothing personal. And they all ended with, 'Best wishes', or 'Good luck'– not even 'Shall be seeing you soon'. But as a card arrived at least every three days I felt that despite everything, and as I had never been spoiled until then either with letters or with anything else, I was being overwhelmed with kindness. Paule was thinking of me on her own account, for Dhuibert never signed any of the cards. It reminded me of our morning walks by the Allier, when we did not say anything very important, but we were together, which was the most marvellous thing in the world. In any case two or three sentences sufficed to fill up the space reserved for correspondence on a postcard. Sometimes even the last words and the signature were written up the side. She had a very tall, pointed writing such as I had never seen before. I admired it for hours in the evenings at home with the snapshots I had taken of her.

During the day I felt the cards in my pocket but forced myself not to take them out and look at them. I worked harder and harder. "Grow up first!" On this score I was quite happy. The business continued to prosper in a miraculous manner and I had never come across such a thing—even in 'Financial Intelligence' at Bloch-Templier's.

The 1st of September came and I still did not know when Paule would return, and the days began to be unbearable. But on the evening of the 3rd, as I returned to my hotel in the rue Caumartin, Fernand the porter told me that a lady had telephoned for me. She would not leave her name or address but said that she would 'phone later.

I went down to dinner with ears cocked, for from the dining-room you could hear the telephone bell if you listened, but I could not swallow a mouthful.

I wondered why Paule had not called me at my office. She must have known that in the superior position I occupied I could receive personal calls. When I asked her later she replied that she had too much respect for my work to disturb me at A.P., Ltd. In any case she did not disturb me any more at the hotel either, and the whole winter, with the exception of this first day, she never telephoned. It was I who called her, and then only on very rare occasions. Dhuibert always fixed our next meeting places when we were together, and nothing was left to chance.

On leaving the table I sat down in the lounge with the papers. What a wait! Normally after dinner I either went to the theatre or up to my room. Since my return from Vichy it was always my room, for to go out without Paule seemed like treachery. But that evening I did not want to put the distance of two floors between myself and the telephone booth.

The lounge struck me as being particularly disagreeable; actually it was only a narrow hall with people coming and going all the time, otherwise I should never have had the courage to sit there, for I should have thought that everyone was looking at me, which was the last thing in the world I wanted. Were it today I should be lying flat on the carpet in the middle of the passage if it could have precipitated Paule's telephone call.

At last, at a quarter to ten: "Hullo, André. Is that you?" It was her voice—that rather metallic strident voice which, according to Dhuibert, was so ingenuous. Her voice! I was so overcome I could not say a word. She must have sensed this, for she said, "So you haven't forgotten me?" and I whispered, "Oh, Paule . . ." Then she asked me if I was free the following afternoon, which was a Saturday. They would expect me at the Hôtel Rembrandt, Avenue Friedland.

I must confess to something which you will perhaps find hard to believe. During the eighteen days we had spent together I knew that Dhuibert and Paule lived in Paris, but neither of them had volunteered their address and I should never have dreamed of asking them. I had become too accustomed in life to asking no questions except those that my work demanded. One must be a man of poise to question one's acquaintances and not always to consider oneself an inferior.

After Paule's telephone call I thought people merely took tea at the Rembrandt as in all the smart hotels round the Etoile. I never imagined they would be living there. On my arrival I was asked my name and requested to go upstairs. Dhuibert had told them at the reception desk that I was coming. So in the lift I found myself back at Vichy, and even more so, as I was now going to visit them in their rooms, which I had never done before. They lived in two huge rooms on the first floor, rather dark on account of the trees in the avenue but magnificently furnished with divan beds. In retrospect the Imperator seemed commonplace.

I went into Dhuibert's room, but I saw Paule's through the communicating door and soon she herself appeared in a black dress which made her look like a great lady. I was awestruck. I thought at the same time: so that's what a real town dress looks like. And then I remembered all the dresses she wore at Vichy—for excursions, for the races and in the evening. And to think that this young girl and no other was willing to be loved by me! But I am not going to begin all that again. . . .

They both gave me a great welcome. They had not changed despite those three interminable weeks. "We have often thought of you," said Paule, and Dhuibert added, "And missed you too—here and there and everywhere. . . ." Everything I had wanted to read between the lines of their postcards was now confirmed. "And so have I . . . you can imagine," I replied with a smile. "We shall have to see a lot of each other," Dhuibert declared. "I imagine you two won't say no to that?"

Paule looked at me with that triumphant smile which showed her teeth and made her look a little predatory. I tried to express in my eyes all the love I felt for her. Dhuibert unfortunately added that they knew a great many people and were very much in demand at the beginning of the season, but that they would be sure to reserve a lot of time for their friend André. I replied, "After office hours I shall be entirely at your disposal."

We had tea and fixed a rendezvous for the following week, for Wednesday evening. I had hoped without breathing a word of it that the following Sunday . . . But they were engaged. That Sunday morning for the first time I entered a florist's. I could not help saying, "I want to send some flowers to my fiancée." The girl replied, "Perhaps you would like a dozen of these beautiful white roses?" A dozen beautiful white roses!

When I arrived at the Rembrandt on Wednesday I learned that they had faded very quickly: but Paule opened one of those boxes made out of an old book and showed me the petals. She plunged her fingers in them.

And then our winter began. I visited the Avenue Friedland two or three evenings a week. Dhuibert often said, "We ought to go to the theatre sometimes." But we never went out, as he insisted he was tired from all the recent dinners and parties. "In any case," he said, "it's very nice to have family evenings like these." And it was, too, with the light on the table and another on the console, the warmth and particularly the perfume—Paule's perfume. It nearly drives me crazy when I think of it.

Dhuibert spoke non-stop of his business, his plans, of conversations with this or that partner—he never gave any names—and I listened to him eagerly. Of course I sometimes regretted our walks in the Allier park, but I told myself that it ought to be like that when it was a question of serious love. In any case there were evenings when I found Paule alone--evenings when Dhuibert returned late and we had a quarter or half an hour to ourselves. "Come and sit here," she would say, and we sat on a little sofa for two side by side, nearer than we had been in the casino at Vichy, for here we were alone. She gave me her hand and I pressed my lips against her soft skin and held them there. Paule ran her hand through my hair and said, "You are a true friend."

At night when I got home I relived these ecstatic moments. I pictured other scenes—holding her in my arms, kissing her lips, caressing her neck and throat, but the moment my imagination tried to go further I heaped reproaches on myself and the next time I saw her I was even more shy because I was so ashamed of having treated her so cavalierly in my dreams.

During the last five autumn days we went out twice in a car. Dhuibert hired one as he had done at Vichy. One Saturday in October we went to Chartres and on All Saints' Day, in magnificent weather, to the forest of Fontainebleau. I already knew Chartres and Fontainebleau also, but only the château and not the forest, as I had been there during the holidays the year before, and in the cathedral I was able to tell them everything about the period and the style. I had never had a chance of speaking at such length in front of Paule. Both she and Dhuibert were astonished. "A scholar and a poet, that's what you are," he said, turning round for confirmation to a group of visitors who had stopped to listen to me. On our return to the hotel . . .

I have not told you why they lived permanently at the Rembrandt. They explained this on the occasion of my first visit. Firstly, with the housing shortage, it was too difficult to find a flat, especially if one was not prepared to accept anything that came along; and then Dhuibert did not wish to inflict the worries of looking after a house upon Paule. He said that a girl would do for a husband what she would not do so willingly for a father. In their position this hotel life suited them much better. On the subject of the hotel I was soon to have a surprise—before our trip to Chartres, about the beginning of October.

One evening as I entered the hall I heard a voice I knew say, "Good evening, M. Gallon." It was Chinchard, the manager of the Imperator. Now that the season at Vichy was over he was managing the Rembrandt. He murmured with a wink and an air of complicity, "I am sure you've come to see our friend Dhuibert." I simply answered yes, very astonished at this change in his behaviour. In any case he had greeted me with as many bows as he used to at Vichy, and later on I saw very little of him because there was not that incessant coming and going at the Imperator which demanded his constant attention.

When I entered Dhuibert's room and was just going to open my mouth he asked: "Have you seen Chinchard? He's just come back from Vichy. Didn't I tell you he was the general manager of the Rembrandt? How foolish of me—but that is the reason why we are living here. I've known Chinchard a long time and have always been very pleased with his services. The Imperator and the Rembrandt belong to the same group, a very important group. The day I come across a block of shares I shall buy them."

After this Dhuibert began to speak of another business that was occupying his attention at that moment and we forgot Chinchard. However, when I returned home that night I thought of it again. They must be in partnership together. Yes, precisely, but I attached no shady significance to this word 'partnership'. It was a few more weeks before I began to wonder. You see, one can be stupid and blinded by love, but when one has been in banking as long as I had there are certain details that cannot be overlooked.

Dhuibert, of course, was always on his guard. He always expressed himself with infinite caution: but for this very reason, this way of never giving away names and remaining vague when it was a question of well-known concerns, of flirting with all sorts of plans which came to nothing, were sufficient proof to me that he was rather a dilettante. Nothing more, I assure you. I never went any further or suspected his honesty or good faith. He continued to be so genial, so simple and so good-humoured. I merely said to myself that he must live rather precariously, dreaming of magnificent enterprises but being content with others far less brilliant, and that he had had his day.

There are many big business men like that, and they cannot all be Rothschilds or Bloch-Templiers. They have a certain flair, a glibness, an ease, and are successful for a few years, and then one fine day luck goes against them. The most provident ones arrange to keep a nice little reserve to assure themselves a peaceful life with cures at Vichy, jewels for their daughters and protracted stays in luxury hotels.

When I began to sum up Pascal Dhuibert in this way I thought I had his measure. This would account for his wanting me to earn more. The money he possessed would perhaps be enough to keep himself and his daughter while he was alive, but after his death . . . And from that moment I ceased to admire Dhuibert and to love him. Yes, to love him.

These genial reflections were born after our trip to Fontainebleau on All Saints' Day in 1927. I had gone to fetch him and found him alone in his room looking very depressed and chewing a cigar. In the corridor I had met Chinchard, who had just left the room and who bowed to me without a word. "What's the matter?" I asked Dhuibert. "Aren't you well?" I had never seen him look so glum. He came over to me and put his hand on my shoulder. "It's nothing, my boy, nothing. I'm only worried." Then after a short silence: "A large block of shares not worth the paper they were printed on. . . . It's hard." He sighed.

I wondered how he could have heard the news as the Stock Exchange was closed for the holiday. I thought that it must be some business of Chinchard's. Then Paule arrived, also looking rather sad. Dhuibert pulled himself together wth an effort. "Let's be off," he said.

As we crossed the hall—he was some way ahead—I whispered in Paule's ear, "Your father is worried." "Be quiet," she said, casting an eye in the direction of Chinchard's office.

During the journey we talked of other things. Dhuibert merely said as we got under way, "It is in difficult moments that one appreciates friends like you, my good André." They don't want to talk, I thought. They haven't enough confidence in me. But I will get it out of them. So I replied, "When the occasion arises, M. Dhuibert, I will give you proof of my friendship."

How will you interpret these pages, Denis? You know, none of the things I've told you before Vichy, of my childhood, of Bloch-Templier, of my mother, really count. It is only now that things are important, and you must pay attention to them if you want to be with me. Other people could tell you about all the rest if need be. And there was the trial. But of the events that follow nobody in the world . . . And the nearer I approach to them the more courage I need to speak of them.

From that day onwards Dhuibert became more and more worried. Paule said to me: "Have you noticed how ill he looks? I am worried. I hear him walking about at night and I'm sure he doesn't sleep. What can we do?" We thought things out together when we were alone, which was more often than before All Saints' Day. From time to time Dhuibert even asked us to go into the next room because he had work to do.

I did not let him notice my joy because of his position, but Paule's bedroom seemed a paradise to me. It was even more bathed in perfume than Dhuibert's room. I could see a dress lying on a chair or a little pair of shoes in the corner which I should have loved to touch.

I should have liked to put flowers everywhere, but Paule had forbidden me, saying: "You mustn't be extravagant,

André. Think of the future." And these words made me sick with happiness. I no longer dared to ask Dhuibert about his business, but I questioned Paule. Each time she replied, "No change, and God knows he is working hard enough," and each time I felt more eager to help them. I said to myself: How wonderful it would be to help them. I, who have really known poverty and hunger. But how? One evening I said to Paule, "You know full well that all my savings are at your father's disposal." She shook my hand replied, "Oh, we haven't got to that point yet—fortunately." But she added, turning her head away, "Not yet. . . ."

And now I too began to pass sleepless nights, thinking out ways and means and inventing schemes—I should never have believed myself capable of so much imagination—but I could find no practical solution. And how could I have done? I knew nothing of the nature of his difficulties.

One Saturday afternoon in December I found him alone as Paule had gone out shopping. He said to me in a pitiful voice: "Tell me, André, tell me how a man who has built huge machines, spas, munition factories, founded real estate companies and who has made millions—do you hear? millions—for himself and others—how can he get into this position—Of course I'm expecting income any day now, but I haven't paid my hotel bill here for November and it worries me, particularly as Chinchard is a pal of mine, and I'd rather die than let a pal down." I replied that his sentiments did him credit but that he must not think of himself alone but of Paule.

I assured him I could lend him the sum he needed without any trouble, but had to persuade him for half an hour before he would accept, and then he agreed only on condition that I did not mention a word to Paule. "She would never forgive me," he said. "She never stops telling me that you are the most generous person in the world, that there is no one like you, and that she has only one fear—that you will get tired of us and our troubles." He fell into a chair and broke down. I wept with him.

That evening I sent him by messenger a cheque for seven thousand francs (made payable to bearer at his request). Four days later, when Paule was not there, he returned the sum to me in cash and embraced me.

Two days after this when I arrived he received me bubbling over with enthusiasm. "Come and let me tell you about my new find," he cried. That day for the first time he spoke to me about the garage. I can still hear him. "My dear André, I think we have got a winner. A magnificent stroke of business which leaped to my eyes yesterday morning as I was going for a walk. Near the Porte de Saint-Cloud, a garage—an enormous garage to hold two or three hundred cars. Not to sell or to buy but to build. That quarter is going to develop considerably and has already begun. Soon the fortification zone will be one single row of buildings, fine buildings for people who like fresh air. You have to be in the money to get fresh air in Paris. Can't you see it now: big industrialists with offices in town, brats with their nurses and naturally motor-cars—motor-cars for us!"

How words can remain engraved in one's mind! And gestures—his little eyes shone again. He was red in the face and happy, thumbs in his waistcoat pockets and his paunch stuck forward. I still did not quite appreciate the value of his idea, but I already began to feel happy too with no other wish than to believe in it. He immediately astounded me by his powers of organization, his energy and keenness, and I even reproached myself for having misjudged him recently. He told me that he had been to see a firm of architects to find out whether they built garages. A single one for ten cars. Then he had compiled a list of the garages in the neighbourhood and had visted them one after another.

He pulled a notebook out of his pocket and read out: "Garage X. Such and such an address, twenty-five cars and three lock-ups. Garage Y, such and such an address, forty cars, no lock-up," and he reeled off seven or eight names and their capacities. "But," he added, "do you know the most important thing? All these garages are full and they have been turning away customers for months . . . so much so that I thought it was impossible that no one else had been struck by the same idea as myself. So I spied out every plot for sale and telephoned the vendors. No options —not even discussions. Then I telephoned to Nice to my friend Bonnefoy and explained the business, and he replied immediately, 'I'm with you.' "

I did not know Bonnefoy, but Dhuibert had often spoken of him. He was an extremely rich man with a château in Touraine and a villa on the Riviera, who had more or less retired from business but who was always ready to support Dhuibert's enterprises, for, it appears, he had pulled off a coup in gold-mining shares which had made him a fortune. During the recent weeks of depression Dhuibert had kept on repeating, "So long as I find a good business Bonnefoy will come in with me, but I've got to find one." And now Bonnefoy, the mysterious Bonnefoy, was 'with him'.

The future once more appeared magnificent and Paule was radiant. That evening I was kept for dinner. We had it in Dhuibert's room and during the whole meal he continued to talk about his plans. During my next visit he added a mass of new information and sketched out the scheme. Finally it became a garage of five storeys for five hundred cars with a ramp and two ten-ton hoists and two lifts. Each car naturally in a lock-up. A repair shop with up-to-date machinery. On the ground floor an enormous showroom, for we were to sell new and second-hand cars as well. On the sixth floor tennis courts open in the summer and heated in the winter, with showers, restrooms, gymnasium and fencing. With a bar restaurant which in summer would be on a terrace with sunshades, flowers and a jazz band. The customers would never want to leave their garage. Dhuibert went into the most minute details, the car-washing, the attendance, the methods of heating and air conditioning. "It must be kept at fifty degrees," he said, "so that the cars don't play us any tricks when they come out into the cold air, and this will also save coal."

He collected estimates, and said: "I know what I'm doing. It's no good their trying to twist me. I must look after the interests of my sleeping partners." Besides, Bonnefoy would not come in unless Dhuibert looked after everything as usual, and agreed to accept the position of managing director, at least for the first year. The price of the land, building and installation would represent an investment of eight to ten millions, but the letting of the lock-ups alone should bring in nearly three million a year—to which would be added the upkeep of the cars, the sales and the profits of the club!

After a week I was as enthusiastic as Dhuibert. I believed everything and agreed to everything. I had been chosen to christen the garage and I christened it *The Garage Paule.* We spent our evenings working out calculations. We had to hurry. Bonnefoy had invited Dhuibert and Paule to spend Christmas in Nice, and Dhuibert had to furnish him with a complete and detailed plan while Curiel, the architect, prepared—according to Dhuibert—the final blueprints. Denis, I can't go on.

When I think of that Christmas and that New Year's

Eve . . . I was alone in Paris and my loneliness was a mixture of joy and despair. I imagined them down there at Bonnefoy's deciding everything, including our future, Paule's and mine. For during the last few days Dhuibert had alluded to it several times and had stopped bothering whether or not I were rich now that this affair was to make him a fortune.

I thought of our future, of our children, and felt so happy that I wished I could have made everybody in the world as happy as myself. I sent toys to the Vinet children and to my typist Mme Corcelles' little boy. On Christmas Eve I sat in my room in front of Paule's photo, looking at it until midnight and, as the clock struck twelve, I wrote, *Paule, will you be my wife?*—a phrase that had been on my lips for weeks—and I wrote it with tears in my eyes. I sent the letter on the following day to the Rembrandt with the inscription "Do not forward" so that she would find it on her return.

That same day—Christmas Day—I went to see the site of The Garage Paule on that barren lot covered with white frost with the same emotion as if I had been going to meet her. Dhuibert had advised me not to speak to anyone in that neighbourhood, and in any case not to mention his name. He had told me that if the affair became known the sharks would be on to it. Who could I have spoken to? On a feast day like this all the neighbouring sites were abandoned and there wasn't a soul to be seen.

I read and re-read the huge board in the middle of the lot: 'For Sale 4,500 Sq. Metres. Apply to . . .' and I told myself that in a fortnight this board would be replaced by another, 'October Next Opening of The Garage Paule, 500 Lock-ups, Tennis, etc.' Yes, everything had to be ready in nine months. "Just the time it takes to produce a baby," he said. Nine months later I was Div. 8, No. 12, in the

Santé! And that's nothing compared with the *image!* There I go rambling again. Each time it comes over me I ought to have the courage to stop and wait for it to pass.

They returned on the 3rd of January, and I, who anticipated radiant faces and also a little emotion on Paule's part because of my letter, was received with funereal gloom. Bonnefoy, it appeared, had only agreed to put up the capital—his and his friends'—for, according to the latest news, his liquid assets did not allow him to subscribe it all—on condition that Dhuibert himself put up at least half a million francs. Dhuibert had naturally agreed, but could realize only a hundred thousand francs at most by selling his remaining shares—all that remained of his capital. "After a blow like this," he said, "there's only one thing for me to do. Disappear. Dhuibert, Pascal Dhuibert, not to honour his bond? It's unthinkable. Bonnefoy is coming to Paris in a few days and I'll be gone. My life is finished. The disgrace! We must go away. . . ."

At that moment I felt that everything had collapsed—a feeling of death, like the night my father caught Maman on the staircase. "You mustn't do that," I cried, and it was Paule who replied, "We must." Then I proposed various solutions. A visit to Bloch-Templier—Dhuibert and myself. The bank would certainly advance a loan straight away. "Against what guarantee?" Dhuibert asked. "I have no collateral. I've been broke for two months. No, this is the end." A desperate man who would not listen to anything.

He sent Paule to her bedroom, and when we were alone looked at me with his terrible little eyes and whispered: "I've told her we shall go away, but it's not true. This is how I'm going. . . ." He pointed his forefinger at his temple. "You will read about it one day in the newspapers. Then you will come and fetch Paule." With teeth chattering I told him he was completely mad, that if Bonnefoy didn't come in with his share he had only to abandon his plan. There would be plenty of others. "I should always need money," he scoffed, "and I should have killed the goose that lays the golden eggs. . . . No, no, it would be poverty for me."

Do you begin to see now. Do you begin to understand? If you could have seen the face he put on—those eyes, that hanging lip beneath his moustache, those clenched hands . . . Three days later Paule left for the country to stay with an aunt. She confided to me that he had forced her to go and that she could not disobey, but she begged me to look after him. Dhuibert, for his part, said, "I'm sending her away." Nothing else, but enough to prevent me from either sleeping or working.

At the office, at my hotel, I waited ceaselessly for a telephone call from the Rembrandt telling me that the tragedy had happened. I went there every evening and found him alternately prostrate, furious or sardonic. He kept repeating, "No one, no one . . ." and I answered, "What about me?" "You!" he replied, "you! You poor thing." His contempt shattered me more than anything else. In front of him I felt as I used to in front of my mother. I said to myself: If he despises me it is because he sees a way out but judges me incapable of using it. He has perhaps spoken about it to Paule. He will kill himself one day and she will be able to accuse me of not having saved her father.

Each time I saw him he grew more distant, less communicative and even hostile. I went through agonies. Until the moment when I said to him: "M. Dhuibert, you have no confidence in me. You think I am a coward." (This was Maman's epithet, and it had haunted me ever since their return from the Riviera.) "You know that I have the means to help, but you will not tell me how because it is certain to be very difficult. Well, I swear to you that nothing could be too difficult for me if it's a question of getting you out of this fix."

He was seated. He got up abruptly—he usually got up rather slowly because of his stature—and looked me hard in the eyes. Then he burst out like a man who can no longer control himself, and spat out all his secret thoughts.

He did not address me directly, did not say to me 'you ought to do this or that'; I can see him now, standing near me, dominating me by his bulk. I was seated at the table. He pointed at me, his eyes more terrifying than ever, and seemed to be accusing me. And I? I listened. I listened to his tirade that was going to turn me into a crook and a rogue. Oh, of course he did not present the thing in that way, and it did not appear like that to me. Of course, I was mad.

Listen, I can't remember all his words in which there was so much anger against me, and so much flattery, so much admiration for 'the anyone else . . . the anyone else in my position'. Here was the plan in a nutshell. And for two days and nights I thought of nothing else.

Through me Dhuibert knew everything there was to know about A.P., Ltd. He knew that the shares had never been printed and that in place of their shares the shareholders merely possessed a holding certificate. He knew, thanks to the confidence of M. Bloch-Templier, my protector, and even from my position in the Company, that I was in the possession of blank certificates signed by M. Maudière. These certificates I held at the disposal of the shareholders in case of need—transfers, sales, etc., and I had only to fill them in before sending them to the parties in question. He knew the names of all the twelve shareholders, their situations, their movements and the number of shares each of them held; during the six months we had known each other we had spoken scores of times, hundreds of times, about A.P., Ltd.; he was always asking me for news of the Company, and as there were no secrets between us I spoke quite openly; in any case even had it been necessary I should never have been able to hide anything from Paule's father.

He knew that one of these shareholders, one of the most important, M. Eskenazi of Eskenazi Shoes, had just left for Buenos Aires on a trip to sound the South American market. He would be away a long time, perhaps a year. M. Eskenazi owned two hundred shares, having a nominal value of two hundred thousand francs, but which, thanks to our phenomenal profits, had risen to ten times that quotation.

We had recently had proof of this and Dhuibert knew it through a transfer of fourteen shares between two members of our group, which had been transacted on the basis of twelve thousand francs per share. Thus Eskenazi's holding of two hundred shares represented a capital of more than two millions. For a loan of two hundred and fifty thousand francs (for Dhuibert did not want more than that, as he said he had come to an arrangement with Bonnefoy) a guarantee of twenty-one shares was all that would be required. With a hundred, anybody in the world would be prepared to advance the money on the spot. 'Anyone else in my place' would take a blank certificate, fill in the name of Eskenazi for a hundred shares and then, with a letter from him, would go and borrow this miserable sum of two hundred and fifty thousand francs. Dhuibert said, "Remember it is only a question of a loan for a few days–for a week at most. A week! Eskenazi will not even have arrived in Buenos Aires. For as soon as I have this sum in my possession Bonnefoy and his friends will put up their shares, and as I am to be in charge of the affair I shall have enough cash to repay the money immediately. Then, out of the first profits, I will liquidate my internal debt to the Company. Nobody will be any the wiser except myself, and I shall be eternally grateful to my rescuer." And I replied: "Nobody except you and M. Eskenazi. We shall have to ask him for that letter to authorize the loan."

Dhuibert flew into a rage. "Are you pretending not to understand?" He rushed to his typewriter, which was in a corner of the room near the window, put a piece of paper in the machine and began to type at an incredible speed. No, at the moment I still had not quite understood and was still waiting to see what would come out of the machine. I was very, very far from realizing what he wanted.

It took him about five minutes. He pulled the paper out violently and came over and waved it under my nose. I know that letter by heart. I had to study it at home all night and to work on it. First of all, in the left-hand corner, *Bordeaux, Jan. 6, 1928* (this was the day Eskenazi had sailed) —then below: *M. André Gallon, Secretary to the Company, A.P., Ltd., 20b rue d'Astorg, Paris. Personal.* Then the text.

My dear Gallon,

As I told you at our last interview I find it necessary that you should send me by return of post, to the address arranged and in cash, the sum of 250,000 francs. I send you therefore by registered post my certificate for a hundred shares, against which you will please obtain for me a loan of this amount on the best terms possible. I rely upon your friendship to do me this service which must remain absolutely confidential. Thanking you in advance and with kind regards, yours sincerely.

Dhuibert had added a postscript: *I enclose a blank receipt signed by me. You will fill it up as required.*

Having read it, I said, "And who is going to sign this letter and the receipt?" Dhuibert seemed to be under great tension. I thought he was going to shout at me, but on the contrary he lowered his voice, but his bloodshot eyes and his clenched fists rendered his reply even more terrible than if he had shouted. And this time he no longer said 'anyone else' but: "Who will sign them? Who? Someone who knows Eskenazi's signature. You–you of course! Are you going to jib at such a trifle when it's a question of saving a man?"

Now at last I understood, and I felt a shiver run down my spine. I wanted to cry out: A forgery. You're asking me to commit forgery; but I simply heard of myself reply, "And who will lend the money on this letter?" A strange gleam came into Dhuibert's eyes. "On the certificate you mean? Anyone–anyone. I could give you ten names."

I began to tremble and the sheet of paper fell to the floor. Dhuibert shrugged his shoulders as Maman used to do. He picked up the letter and sat down with his head in his hands. Suddenly I realized that my eyes were fixed on Paule's door, and my heart, my whole body, leaped. "I'll do it," I whispered. Dhuibert did not move. "I'll do it," I said in a louder voice. He turned a strained and anxious face towards me. "You'll do it?" he said. "You'll have the heroism to do it?" He stressed the word 'heroism'. "Yes," I repeated, "I'll do it. Now let me go." I took the letter and stuffed it in my pocket.

Dhuibert's eyes followed my movements. I believe he was thinking: Go? Why? and I'm sure at that minute he was frightened. But actually I was only thinking of my heroism. I thought of it the whole night following our conversation, the whole of the next day in the office and the whole of the next night. I thought I could become a hero by copying a signature, by making a false certificate and giving a false receipt. I told myself that heroism consisted in risking something for others and not for oneself.

After all, was that so stupid? I said that if I were discovered I should have sacrificed myself for Paule, for her father, for love. In any case I was sure I should not be found out, not only because of the fact that the plan was almost foolproof but that fate would not allow me to be punished for an heroic gesture.

The next night I prayed. I don't know to whom or to what, but I prayed. "I must do that, mustn't I?" I said. Ah, Denis, if God exists that was the moment for Him to intervene. A God Who would have known the whole truth; but there is no God, and I repeated to myself: Yes, I must do it. But don't imagine that on the second day this did not make me feel terrible in front of M. Maudière and even the employees in the bank, down to the office boy; and when M. Bloch-Templier telephoned during the day I was almost incapable of answering him.

But what a compensation that evening at the Rembrandt with Dhuibert! He had waited forty-eight hours for me and when I saw him sitting in exactly the same place as I had left him one would have said he had not stirred the entire time. I sat down beside him, took his hand and comforted him. I asked him who would advance us the money.

He seemed to reflect, and began by suggesting certain banks, banks I had never heard of. Then he changed his mind. It would be better to go to a moneylender who specialized in loans against guarantees, for example a certain Lévêque in the rue du Château-d'Eau. Naturally Dhuibert's name must not appear and he insisted that I should make no reference to him whatsoever. He told me that one day he had got the better of Lévêque in a deal and the fellow had never forgiven him; but since that time he was on the level and one could work with him in all confidence. And he had the means.

I promised to go and see him as soon as possible. We spoke in undertones and I felt very close to him. Dhuibert put his arm round my shoulder and said: "My son—you really are my son. We will wire the news to our Paule." He took a piece of paper and saying that he would copy it later on a telegraph form wrote: *Paule D. Saved by André. Everything fine.*

I left him soon afterwards. In the corridor I thought I had left something behind. I did not quite know what. Perhaps I was eager to hear more words of enthusiasm and affection. I retraced my steps and pushed upon the door. Dhuibert was burning a piece of paper in the flame of a candle. He started as he saw me. It was the telegram. "You must forgive me," he said quickly; "I thought I'd better wait until the business was finished before telling her. I am so unlucky these days." I nodded approval, but I felt rebellious. "You will be able to wire her tomorrow," I said. And then another sleepless night.

The next morning I telephoned to Lévêque from an inconspicuous café which I had finally discovered in the rue Saint-Philippe-du-Roule. A woman's voice made an appointment for me for the following evening at seven o'clock. I still had two days and one night to kill—one night to practise imitating a signature.

I had taken home some of Eskenazi's letters, old correspondence of no importance that would not have been missed from his private file if by any chance someone had consulted it. I spent hours and hours at this task and concentrated so deeply that I forgot my reason for doing it. It reminded me of having to draw a picture of the mountains in charcoal at the *lycée*. Eskenazi, réné eskenazi, all in small letters, even the initials, and three parallel, almost vertical, lines for the flourish.

I was fairly successful at the start and after a while became perfect. I filled up a certificate for a hundred shares and prepared a blank receipt. Friday evening, on leaving the office, I went to find Lévêque. I kept saying to myself, So long as I don't meet anybody.

I chose very small back-streets as ill-lit as possible, but I was trying to observe the people I passed beneath the street lamps. My cheeks were on fire and the words kept turning over and over in my head: It's for Paule. I even spoke to her familiarly as I walked. It is for you, Paule; for you, my beloved. Despite the cold the sweat ran down between my shoulder blades.

I found myself in front of an old house with a dark, narrow staircase, No. 28 rue du Château-d'Eau. Here I am, I thought, and the sweat froze on my back. However, it was all so amazing that I don't want to go too fast. What a pretty document this makes! I hope for your sake you won't often have occasion to receive such confessions. And then, if he comes back now before I've finished, I shall only have to jot down a sentence, a simple word, and you will have grasped it all—the image, the obsession, my silence, my last gesture.

How curious—this morning I wondered how I should ever have the courage to write, and now I want to take my time, not to skip anything. Actually I am happy at the moment. I cannot explain why. I already seem to be aiming at him. Yes, that's it—my vengeance has begun.

Through a half-open door on the third floor a young girl asked me if I had an appointment. Then she showed me into a waiting-room and opened a leather door in the wall. I heard her saying, "It's the gentleman who telephoned." She returned and sat down at her typewriter. She typed very slowly, much slower than my typist or Dhuibert.

The room must have looked out on to the back, for there was not a sound except the tapping of the keys. The furniture consisted of a small filing cabinet and a few chairs upholstered in old leather, as worn as that of the door. A lamp with a green shade gave a poor light and there was a smell of burning. How well I remember! This is because the noise of the typewriter and the smell had put my nerves on edge and I was thinking: Two hundred and fifty thousand francs in a place like this?

I did not have long to wait. A bell rang and the girl got up to open the door for me. I found myself in front of M. Lévêque, a fat little bald man wearing his war ribbons. He came towards me and after a glance at my clothes his face expanded. Pointing to a chair, he said politely: "Sit down, monsieur. What can I do for you?" Not even the typewriter could be heard here, but there was still the smell of burning.

M. Lévêque sat down in turn and repeated, "What can I do for you?" Until then I had feared a reception such as we reserved at Bloch-Templier's for casual borrowers. But obviously there was no connection at all. I was not in the least intimidated. In any case, I thought, I have not come on my own account, but for Eskenazi. So I came out with my story, which I had prepared with the rest. The more I spoke the more my self-assurance increased. I, the general secretary of Adams Process, Ltd., had been commissioned by one of our shareholders, with whom incidentally I happened to be on the most friendly terms, etc., etc. Lévêque listened to me and picked his cuticles.

When I mentioned A.P., Ltd., he raised his eyebrows with sudden interest. I showed him the letter and he read it carefully. Then he said, "Isn't your own company with all its wealth, prepared to advance this sum to oblige one of its shareholders?" The fact that he knew our reputation gave me even more confidence. I replied that A.P., Ltd., refused to undertake any operations of that kind and that besides, as he had written in his letter, M. Eskenazi wanted the matter kept secret—'for family reasons' I added—and furthermore did not want to approach a recognized loan society.

I must have blushed at that moment, but Lévêque was not looking at me. He had also turned red and said, "But who gave you the idea of coming to me?" I quoted a name which Dhuibert had given me and mentioned a business in which Lévêque, it appeared, had been of great service.

He gave a little laugh of satisfaction and said immediately, "Will you excuse me a minute?" and asked for a telephone number. The conversation began with a "Is that you?" and after a few courtesies: "I have a gentleman in my office who is discussing A.P., Ltd., 20b rue d'Astorg, with me. . . . Naturally, I know that, but can you give me a few precise details?"

From that moment he never said a word. He merely listened. He tried to look disinterested because I was there but did not succeed. He grew scarlet to the top of his head, which he shook from time to time with little exclamations. Obviously he was being given details about A.P., Ltd., which were enough to amaze anyone. He made a few notes on his writing-pad.

After he had hung up he told me that it was not too easy to lay one's hands on two hundred and fifty thousand francs, but I realized that he was speaking more for his own benefit than for mine. Nevertheless the business seemed straightforward enough to him and that was the only kind of business he liked.

He asked me to give him until Monday to collect additional information. I told him that not only did I grant (I actually said grant!) this delay, but that I hoped he would come to A.P., Ltd., so that I could furnish him with the information myself and show him the necessary documents, including M. Eskenazi's certificate, which I kept in my safe. This was not true: it was in my pocket-book.

I suggested an appointment for Monday morning, for M. Maudière never came to the office on Mondays. He was voluble in his thanks and called me *Monsieur le Secrétaire Général* as he accompanied me to the door.

I had so little expected a reception of this kind that I left with an enormous desire to laugh. Not out of cynicism, Denis. Don't forget I was convinced we should be paying back the loan within a very short time. However, this man, who was going to allow me to save two lives—three, actually, for I knew life would mean nothing to me without Paule—seemed even happier than all of us and more than anxious to do the business. He had said to himself, of course—he repeated it at the trial—M. Eskenazi will obviously pay me back (don't forget I had also told him it was M. Eskenazi, and he needed no information about the Eskenazi Shoe Company), but even if he does not pay me back I hold in my hands a security worth more than a million francs. Instead of selling to reimburse this loan I shall keep the shares and become a shareholder in A.P., Ltd., in a company that has doubled its capital in two years and which goes from strength to strength.

That night I slept, Denis, but I do not think that the same can be said for Lévêque, for he telephoned me next morning at the rue d'Astorg to ask if he could not come and see me straight away. Without thinking I replied, "Of course." Then I waited for him in terror.

Maudière had not yet arrived, but he nearly always passed through my office to say good morning before going to his own. It is true that whenever I had a visitor he closed the door again and went straight along the corridor to his own room. But afterwards he always asked me who the visitor was—or rather I told him—for I had never received anyone at A.P., Ltd., except on business. Half an hour later he telephoned to say he had a touch of 'flu and would stay at home for the day. I felt that this piece of luck was a happy omen.

Lévêque spoke to me even more respectfully than he had done in the rue du Château-d'Eau. He was clutching a small black portfolio under his arm, but this did not prevent him from nibbling at his nails. Naturally our building, our impressive office, the manner in which he had been received by being asked to write his name and being told that *M. le Secrétaire Général* would see him in a few moments, offered him all the proofs he needed. However he did not neglect his guarantees on this account. I showed him the Articles of the Company, the share register in which he could see M. Eskenazi's name—and that he held not one hundred but two hundred shares—the balance-sheets and other documents.

Once more I had forgotten the forgeries and the forged certificate and I thought only of presenting A.P., Ltd., in its most favourable light as a good servant of the Company.

Lévêque nodded, quite convinced. He could not be anything else. There were ten documents to certify the accuracy of each of my statements. It also came out in this conversation that I was in a good position. As M. Maudière used to say, "Second in command to God . . . God being myself."

Lévêque apologized for keeping me so long and drew out of his portfolio two hundred and fifty thousand francs in banknotes—five bundles of fifty notes. I was so surprised to see them appear—I imagined that I should have to return to the rue du Château-d'Eau—that my hands trembled, but he did not notice. He was thinking only of displaying his gratitude.

He explained to me that he had done the necessary to collect the sum as soon as the bank opened, not without some difficulty. But he had not forgotten that in his letter M. Eskenazi wanted to obtain this advance by return of post. He asked me almost timidly if I thought twelve per cent interest would be excessive. "You see," he said laughingly, "I can hardly expect M. Eskenazi to default, and so . . ." As he foresaw an advance for six months the interest would amount to fifteen thousand francs. I told him that he would be paid back long before that, perhaps in a month or a fortnight, but that I fully understood that he could not agree to a transaction for a shorter period. Dhuibert had said to me, "Accept whatever he asks." He had foreseen far more usurious terms.

We then exchanged receipts: Lévêque acknowledging that he held M. Eskenazi's share certificate as guarantee for a loan of two hundred and sixty-five thousand francs, and I—or rather Eskenazi—giving him the counterpart. We counted the money and I thanked him. "Not at all, not at all," he replied. "I have to thank you for having brought me the business."

You should have seen his face at the investigation and at the trial. . . . But we must be patient. To think that just now I wanted to take my time, and now I am going from one extreme to the other. My writing-pad is coming to an end: no more than a couple of dozen sheets left. I must go out and buy another at once, for it's getting late, and a new week begins tomorrow which should bring him here. From tomorrow morning I must hold myself in readiness. I must have finished. One afternoon and one night left.

(*A little later.*)

THE TWO paper-shops here are shut on Sundays, but my tobacconist had a few blocks—sky blue, my friend, exactly the right paper for a prospective angel and future candidate for paradise, whose gates are already open. It is on sky-blue paper that I am going to speak to you of . . . Magnificent. Who is the terrible demon who makes a mockery of us like this? . . . More philosophy! Of us? No, of me, of me alone: nobody could ever have lived a life like mine.

It is wonderful weather—still fresh from this morning's rain. "Do you mean to say you work in this weather," the tobacconist said to me, "instead of going for a walk?" The main street was crowded. People were buying cakes in the pastrycook's. I heard a bell ring in the cinema behind the Café du Commerce—the end of the film, I suppose. Only his house looks dead. Have they gone out for the day? Or won't they allow the children in the garden because it's damp underfoot? They are wrong: there's nothing to fear on gravel, for the rain sinks into the ground and it is not like a lawn. Children ought to run about in the open air all day, rain or fine. If they get wet they can be given a rub down afterwards. I should have known how to bring up children. Oh yes, it's all very well to talk about children!

A company secretary has just received money from a moneylender, which he has procured on a loan against shares —that's where we got to, isn't it? Now that the business was finished and I had the two hundred and fifty bank-notes, I seemed to have embarked upon a new life, to have changed my spots. I was surprised. Yes, tremendously surprised.

I said to myself as I walked along (I returned home with

the money, as I did not have to see Dhuibert before the evening, and he did not imagine the affair was already in the bag, as I had not expected a visit from Lévêque until Monday), "I've really done it!" And as the world had not changed at all it was I who did not recognize myself. I was a hero, a hero and a rogue, no connection therefore with the Gallon boy who had never dreamed of becoming either the one or the other; for there is a great gulf between dreaming of being a hero and becoming one. And now there was no more gulf. I had acted, acted for the one I loved.

I had the joy of being received by Paule, although I thought she was still away, and Dhuibert said to me, "I wanted her here to give you courage for Monday." I handed him my portfolio and he took the bundles of notes out himself. If you could have seen their faces. How I trembled when Dhuibert cried: "But give him a kiss, my girl. Thank him yourself for having saved my life!" She gave me her hand. I did not stir. I looked at her in amazement. She smiled with a trace of embarrassment and murmured, "Thank you, André." Dhuibert slapped me on the back and said: "Well, kiss each other, come along! Don't engaged couples kiss any more?" This was the first time that the word had been uttered officially. She offered me her cheek and I barely touched it with my lips. Well, never mind.

Our engagement. . . . Nothing changed very much. Dhuibert asked me to keep it secret: he wanted to get into his stride. We went out together no more than before, and I spent no more time in Paule's bedroom than before, but as, since New Year's Day, I had been deprived of this happiness, it appeared to me new and marvellous. However, I never kissed her again after the evening I have just spoken to you about, for I felt she was nervous and on her guard as soon as I wanted to be demonstrative. At first I said to her, "You don't love me, Paule," and she replied with some irritation "Of course I do, of course I do, but I'm like that." And I, who worshipped everything about her, accepted everything.

I had never known a society girl before and I thought that they never allowed themselves to be ruled by their feelings, for all the same she occasionally gave me proof of some sentiment. Once she said to me, for instance, "You're so intelligent, André, and above all you're so good. I've never met a man like you before," and she said it looking straight into my eyes as though she really meant it; and one day—I'm not very good-looking, Denis—she said that she thought me attractive. This overwhelmed me. Yes, far more than when she spoke of my brain or my good heart. Vanity. . . . Another day she remarked, "You have the eyes of a man who has faith," and I replied, "Yes, faith in you." And then she ran her hand through my hair with an absentminded gesture.

I repeat, I should often have been anxious had I not accepted everything about her; and then, I attributed the shadows that passed across her lovely face to Dhuibert's troubles. Sometimes I found her looking so disgusted with life that she did not seem the same person, but as soon as she saw me she at least smiled, and I told myself that I was a consolation and a support to her. My gesture had proved it.

At the end of January, after a couple of weeks of enthusiasm, Dhuibert had begun to give us indifferent news. He had lost his triumphant expression and his energy. There were difficulties in getting The Garage Paule Company formed. Bonnefoy raised more and more objections, and what was even more serious, the prices envisaged at the end of 1927 had risen considerably.

The day Dhuibert told me this he added, "It's lucky we

have a breathing space with Lévêque." I told him in terror that it was not a question of Lévêque but of Eskenazi. At this he grew very angry and assured me that at the least alarm he could always replace the money, but with things as they were, he would prefer not to be forced to do so. The rise in the estimated costs demanded all our available liquid assets.

And then I began to be really anxious. I though that Dhuibert was truly out of luck, but at the same time I gradually began to lose faith in him—still not in the sense that you think, as I should have done. I merely wondered if he grasped the grave situation and if he realized what would happen to us in five months if . . . I pulled myself together and consoled myself with the thought that in five months the great project of the garage would be launched.

I'm not going to tell you everything that went through my mind. What use would it be? I tried to confide in Paule, but she interrupted me as soon as I started and begged me to spare her the details. She told me that he could not bear to be contradicted at the moment and that his difficulties had put him into a terrible state of nerves.

I became aware of this at my next visit. I always asked him as soon as I arrived, "Well, what's the news?"—a habit I had got into during the happy period when the idea of the garage had first arisen. Since then the situation had grown steadily worse, and on the evening of which I am speaking my voice trembled as I said the words.

Dhuibert flew into a terrible rage, a really brutal rage. I was alone with him, for Paule had gone to bed. She'll come in, I thought. She won't allow him to treat me like this. But there was no sign of her and I said to myself, She's too afraid; she's like me, too afraid. I could imagine her with her head beneath the bedclothes and her hands over her ears.

I was thinking so much of her that I hardly heard Dhuibert's insults. For they were real insults. Horrible words he used—that I was the most grasping, the most Jesuitical man he had ever met and that I thought of nothing but my money while he was killing himself with work and worry to assure Paule's future and mine. "A gesture? You have never made a gesture in your life!" he screamed, with a contemptuous movement of his hand.

He jeered at my poor, narrow little life; he taunted me with all the confidences I had given him, with all the little things Paule did not know about me, and which she was perhaps hearing at this moment. He's mad, I thought, and thought I was going mad myself. No one had ever abused me like that since my mother, and then with Maman it was quite different.

I had already seen Dhuibert in violent tempers, but never like this. He was standing near the fireplace and kept banging his fist on the marble, and after each phrase he hiccoughed as though he were really going to vomit up his bile. At last he cried, "And now you can get out!" I was completely cowed. I put my hands together and said: "You can't do that. You can't possibly drive me away." I cried for mercy, do you understand, as I had done to Palaiseau and Bruneval. Oh, I fully realized all his injustice, but in the next room lay all my life, my love. . . . He swayed to and fro for a moment, took a cigar out of his pocket, bit the end off with a noise that broke the silence and said at length, hardly less harshly than all his previous horrors: "Good night. Things will be better tomorrow."

As I left I kept repeating to myself: I've lost Paule. I shall never dare return tomorrow. I've lost Paule. At that moment I cared nothing for Lévêque or Eskenazi or anything. I walked for an hour and remained sitting in my chair until morning. But when I left the hotel to go to the office the porter handed me a note. Four words: *Until this evening. Paule.* How I counted the hours!

I found an anxious, frowning Paule. Dhuibert hardly gave me his hand. He declared that our discussion the night before had made him ill and had prevented him from being in form that afternoon at a conference about the new company. They wanted to bring in a co-director but, worst of all, he had just had a letter from Bonnefoy, the contents of which he read out as though flinging them in my face. The letter reminded him that, as he had taken on the responsibility for the estimates, it was up to him personally to furnish the difference between the original and the increased costs, a matter of four hundred thousand francs. In default of this Bonnefoy and his partners considered the affair null and void and he alone would have to bear the expenses already incurred—the option on the land and formation of the company.

He kept repeating furiously: "Alone. I'm alone!" But Paule flung herself in his arms and cried: "No. No, you're not alone."

I should have said to myself, shouldn't I, that the man who had written the letter from Eskenazi could also have written the one from Bonnefoy? Obviously. There were so many things I ought to have realized, but I did nothing of the sort; for Dhuibert, with his arms round Paule, told me that he intended to resign and to return me the two hundred and fifty thousand francs. As regards the expenses incurred he would let the creditors sue him as he was bankrupt. "Your father will go to prison," he said to Paule. She fled into her bedroom. "To prison," he repeated. This time he did not mention suicide. "Never!" I replied.

I hope I have not done anything stupid. I rang for the chambermaid and told her that I did not feel very well and that I preferred not to go down to dinner. To go through all the same business as at midday . . . no, thank you! I asked her to bring me a large jug of coffee and some bread. I shan't eat the bread because I'm not hungry, but the coffee will put some heart into me and I need it. My temples are throbbing and my eyes burning from having written so much—almost two hundred pages. It will soon be time to start on the sky-blue paper. You who have studied graphology . . . I wonder what you will find in my handwriting? Does it show that I am at least capable of one great deed?

I am going to lie down and wait for my coffee.

(*A little later.*)

I REPLIED, "Never!" I understood his violence and his despair so well. I said to myself that I was the victim because one was necessary, and that doubtless . . . Well, what of it? I replied, "Never!" and that's that. As I said that word I saw our share register: "M. Réné Eskenazi, 200 shares." Lévêque had one hundred: someone else might just as well have the other hundred. If a hundred shares represented more than a million francs I could just as easily get a loan of four hundred thousand francs against them as two hundred and fifty thousand.

I said as much to Dhuibert of my own accord without being asked. He listened to me until I had finished without saying a word, and then he fell on his knees in front of me. He fell on his knees in front of me!

Yes, I am nearing the end, Denis. Perhaps I shall not even

need my sky-blue paper. I don't know if it's the coffee but I suddenly feel very well, very good-humoured and in great form to tell you the story of the four hundred thousand francs. Do you remember it? I was given headlines and two columns on the front page in the newspapers. The secretary who placed four hundred thousand francs in front of his director, saying: "Take them. I've stolen them." After that we shall have come full circle. There is very little left before we get there—practically nothing to tell, a mere straw. . . . Now I am very calm and you shall hear it all. I've still time to write a little. I have got to be prepared to leave tomorrow morning. Prepared? Yes, for him.

First of all I must tell you how I procured the four hundred banknotes. The newspapers reported that too. But I'm perfectly entitled to recount my great deeds myself. I am the star, and the more celebrated a star becomes and the more the public knows of his life the more personal appearances are requested of him. Ladies and gentlemen, this is how I proceeded: naturally the inspiration again came from the honourable M. Pascal Dhuibert.

In the autumn I had told him (and he remembered—he remembered everything, the big rogue) that I had had a visit from a very important person with a high-faluting name, M. Perret de la Barre. This Perret de la Barre had begun by writing to A.P., Ltd., asking whether we had any shares on offer. I had replied in the negative, and informed him that in view of the way the business was progressing our shareholders very naturally wished to retain their interests. Despite my letter M. Perret de la Barre had paid us a visit and I had received him as part of my normal routine. He was more than keen to buy, irrespective of price, and had even proposed giving me a commission the day I could oblige him.

That evening, or on the following day, I mentioned this

to Dhuibert because I had never met anyone so importunate. I had forgotten all about his visit—not so Dhuibert. Furthermore he told me a few days later that M. Perret de la Barre had enormous funds at his disposal and used them to the full advantage.

When I congratulated Dhuibert on his sources of information he replied: "Always be inquisitive, Gallon, always be inquisitive. With inexhaustible curiosity and a sound memory . . . I get these tips to be of service to you should the occasion arise." Well, the occasion had now arisen: he brought up the name of Perret de la Barre. We repeated the trick of Eskenazi's letter and I asked for an appointment.

What has come over me? Why am I telling it to you in this manner? Why do I want to make you believe in my cynicism? I am coming to the moment which destroyed my whole existence, which made life impossible, which within the next twenty-four or forty-eight hours will result in two deaths, and yet this is the moment I choose to deceive you about myself. Coffee and brandy . . . they are not the right diet for dying people. No, Denis, I had not suddenly become a rogue. I acted the second time just as the first, but with even more emotion and love.

I must tell you that after my proposal, when I had raised Dhuibert to his feet, he overwhelmed me with words and promises, asked my forgiveness and swore that now everything was definitely saved. He even gave me precise dates for repayment. Don't forget that he had just offered to return the two hundred and sixty-five thousand francs for Lévêque, and above all, above all, he had spoken of marriage. As soon as everything was completed the engagement would be announced officially and the marriage could take place a fortnight later. We would invite Block-Templier, Maudiére, Bonnefoy, and a host of other people.

Dhuibert wanted to leave the Rembrandt as soon as possible

and hire an apartment where we could celebrate the engagement. Paule had remained in her bedroom and I was dying to call her in so that she could hear these wonderful plans, but Dhuibert told me: "She has been so upset recently. I had better tell her myself later. It will be better."

He repeated his manœuvre and sent her away the following morning so that I should not see her, and that I should desire her even more. This time he left Paris to join her. He assured me that her nerves were so bad that he feared she would have a breakdown. He intended to nurse her outside Paris just as long as it took to arrange everything.

They chose the Hôtel des Reservoirs, at Versailles. "When you've finished the business you can telephone and we'll return immediately," he added. We parted that evening on the pavement in the Avenue Friedland in front of the Rembrandt. He disappeared, muffled up in his great overcoat, into a taxi. It was bitterly cold. I looked at the hotel, that huge, empty building, which no longer housed either Paule or Dhuibert. I thought: We must hurry. I telephoned Perret de la Barre . . . another night spent on the certificate and the letter.

M. Perret de la Barre received me like an old acquaintance in his luxurious apartment in the rue Lincoln. He offered me cigarettes and asked me if I liked painting, and showed me his gallery. We passed a young, very over-scented, red-haired young lady with freckles—not in the least pretty. He introduced me as if I were somebody important, "My daughter." Then we returned to his study.

I felt far less at ease with him than with the money-lender of the rue du Château-d'Eau. I said to myself: Supposing he knows Eskenazi personally! I let slip the name, but obviously he did not know him, and this gave me courage.

I explained everything to him. M. Eskenazi wanted a

loan in absolute confidence of four hundred thousand francs. This loan would be repaid, of course, but if it was not, M. Perret de la Barre would be the possessor of the block of shares he wanted so much. In fact, I said to him everything which Lévêque had turned over in his mind. I apologized for bringing him such a hypothetical business—a chance in a thousand—but I remembered his visit and I wanted to see him benefit by this slender opportunity. A fine lie, eh? Can you imagine: to seduce him more effectively I had written on the receipt: *In default of repayment on the above mentioned date of expiration* [I had put three months this time] *I agree that the sum in question be considered as the outright purchase price of forty shares* [which put each share at ten thousand francs when they were worth twelve thousand] *valid on the share certificate attached, etc.* I had even written: *It being understood in this case that the present receipt is valid as discharge for the said purchase, and that I will do all in my power to agree to this transfer by my co-partners.*

M. Perret de la Barre replied that if Eskenazi did not repay him he would take the liberty of offering me a thousand francs for each share he could retain; i.e. forty thousand francs. I cut him short by telling him that even had I been prepared to accept his offer, which was far from my thoughts, I was certain that I should never be in a position to collect the money. He seemed quite delighted anyhow, and was very complimentary.

We discussed the question of interest. This did not seem to bother him, and we fixed five per cent. Thereupon he told me that he had not got that amount in cash but that if I would take a cheque he would notify the bank and I could collect it immediately. I grew a little distrustful. Did not so open an offer conceal some trap? I replied that M. Eskenazi's certificate was in my safe and begged him to come to the rue d'Astorg. I had suddenly become so optimistic that I did not even worry about a possible meeting with Maudière. Naturally Perret de la Barre would not have said a word which might have involved Eskenazi's honour. . . .

How simple it all was, Denis! If my cheeks had not been on fire and my hands moist I should really have felt at my ease. That is how one steals. But I repeat once more: I did not think I was stealing. I was sure I was not stealing. I saw myself bringing back the money into this same office, collecting the certificate and tearing up the receipt. And no one any the wiser. I should marry Paule and we should have children, and they would never be obliged to have recourse to such practices.

He brought me the money at five o'clock that afternoon. It was a Thursday, Thursday, the 12th of February, my last day but one. Four hundred thousand francs in forty bundles of ten. I nearly telephoned to Versailles, but then made up my mind that it would be nicer to surprise them. Dhuibert had been so happy on the first occasion when I had brought him the money two days before he expected it. The next day I asked M. Maudière for the day off. He smiled and wished me a pleasant holiday. I could not help blushing. "Could this debauch," he added, "possibly be a prelude to some serious engagement?" M. Maudière spoke well and liked to be witty. Despite Dhuibert's advice I let the words escape, "It could be, monsieur." He shook his head and declared that with a serious boy like me one wouldn't expect anything else. At the same time he held out his hand and added, "Every good wish, my young friend." I did not reply, but shook his hand so hard that he winced, and then I went back to my office to collect my portfolio in which I had put the money.

Directly after dinner I went up to my bedroom. I had

no forebodings, Denis. On the contrary, I had more confidence in the future than I had ever previously experienced. I did not close my eyes all night. I thought of Vichy, of my first dreams when Paule had appeared so very inaccessible to me. And I held her naked in my arms. . . . I had often dreamed of this during the winter, but now I felt that the dream would soon become fact, very soon indeed. I was going to earn the right to take her, possess her and make her mine. I groaned aloud with happiness and I am sure that through those cardboard walls the neighbours must have thought I was not alone.

On the following morning at nine o'clock I set out for the Invalides with my portfolio. If only people knew, I thought, that it's stuffed full of banknotes! But nobody paid any attention to me *yet*. On my arrival at Versailles, where everything appeared dead with cold, I thought that perhaps it was too early to arrive unexpectedly.

I went into a café near the station and telephoned to the Reservoirs. Dhuibert was on the other end of the line, his voice still thick with sleep. I told him I had the documents we needed and that I wished to bring them to him so that he need not return to Paris. "Splendid idea," he replied. "Of course. Try and get free and come to lunch with us. Don't have yourself announced. Say that you are expected in No. 64. I must go now so as not to wake Paule up, and thanks to you I can get a little peaceful sleep." I hung up, laughing heartily. He had been under the impression that I was telephoning from Paris and I did not bother to enlighten him. I could really give him a surprise now.

I asked the way to the Hôtel des Reservoirs, turned up my coat collar and set out. I was there at five minutes to ten. I said that I was expected, gave the number of the room and was allowed to go upstairs. Being certain that Dhuibert was asleep, I did not even knock, but pushed the door open gently and slipped my head round. The bed was turned down and empty. I went into the room and shut the door behind me without making a sound. The communicating door was also shut. I went towards it, thinking, Paule is awake, Dhuibert must have gone to tell her the news.

Then I began to hear noises and voices, meaningless voices which groaned and breathed heavily—the voices of Paule and Dhuibert and the creaking of a bed. And the groans and the breathing grew louder and louder. I felt my jaw begin to tremble and I had a strangling feeling in my throat as though I were being hanged. I hurled myself at the door and tried the handle. It was locked. There was a silence that lasted maybe a fraction of a second, maybe more; I don't know. Then Dhuibert called out in a hoarse voice, "Who is it?"

"Open the door," I roared, "or I'll break it in!"

Paule whispered, but I heard her as if my ear had been pressed to her lips. I heard Dhuibert say: "All right, I'm coming. Wait a minute, André. Paule's ill."

I began shouting again and banging on the panel with my fists. "Open, or I'll break down the door!" Dhuibert shouted angrily, "Keep quiet, you idiot!" but I went on banging and crying: "Open the door! Open the door!" He was wearing his pyjama top but not the trousers. He had grabbed them on the way and held them in front of him rolled in a ball to cover his nakedness. He gave me a thunderous look.

Now that the door was open I could not move. I stood there with my hat on my head, my collar turned up and the portfolio under my arm. I could see nothing but his eyes, and yet at the same time I could distinguish Paule in her bed with the clothes drawn up to her chin. I don't know what I must have looked like, but Dhuibert suddenly lost his head.

Perhaps he had expected me to attack him, and this is what I had had in mind, but I could not do it. I was powerless. I felt that I had just undergone a torture, that I had been branded with red hot irons which had paralysed me and left me nothing but an image burned into my retina—that great naked man with his jacket open, showing his hairy chest and legs and that swab of stuff pressed between his thighs. With his other hand he seized me by the arm, dragged me into the room and shut the door.

He took advantage of being behind me to slip on his pyjama trousers, saying to Paule at the same time: "Explain to him! We can explain . . . go on, explain!" Now I was at the foot of Paule's bed, but I could still see Dhuibert. He had taken off my hat and was trying to remove the portfolio. He could not do it, but I know that I never moved when he tried. He pushed me down on a chair and I fell into it. It was quite simple: I no longer existed.

Then the great scene began, the final scene. He was facing me with his knees against mine. He explained to me that Paule was not his daughter but his niece and ward, and that he had seduced her when she was still a little girl; but that since Vichy he had never touched her again because she would not have allowed it, because she loved me; but that morning, knowing I was coming and that he was going to lose her for ever, he could not resist for the last time. . . . He kept repeating: "That's right, isn't it, Paule? Isn't it?" and Paule replied, "Yes," from beneath the clothes. I still did not move. I kept seeing him standing there naked with his clout. And Dhuibert went on and on.

He spoke very quickly and from time to time put out a hand towards my knee or towards my shoulder, but drew it back again because he was afraid. "My boy," he said, "we're not going to turn back now on account of a misunderstanding. The garage affair has gone west. Everybody's dropped it and I shall never be able to repay the money. We'll all three of us flee to Belgium. With the four hundred notes that you've brought we can look around."

I did not feel capable of moving, and yet Paule cried out: "I'm frightened, Papa, I'm frightened. Look how he's mocking us!" Yes, she actually said Papa! Dhuibert's face grew even redder and he came closer and threatened me in a low voice. I could feel his breath. "Look," he said, "it's no good trying to impress me with this frigid English air. You don't scare me, you know. All right, I've been good enough to suggest that we all go together. If you don't want to, all right. I'll leave you in the lurch."

Suddenly I found myself standing up. "André, you're not going to denounce us!" cried Paule. Dhuibert stood up too. "Let him go ahead," he said with a leer. "What's he got on me, eh? Did I force him to swindle people? Has he any proof, I ask you? Has he a single proof?" I looked towards Paule. She was sitting up in bed but she had kept the clothes over her breasts and was looking at me with terrified eyes. "Say something, André," she moaned. "Don't go away. Don't go away. I . . . I . . ."

I could still see Dhuibert standing there with his pyjamas between his thighs. He ran towards the bed and cried: "Yes, tell him you love him. Tell him you love him, and show him how beautiful you are." He tore the sheet out of her hands and I saw Paule stark naked with her hands still clenched above her breasts. At that moment the image of Dhuibert disappeared and I saw her clearly—yes, in every detail.

"Look at that," Dhuibert cried. "See how beautiful she is." I clutched my portfolio in my left hand and with my right, as he had his back to me, I pushed him with all my might. He fell on top of her. At last I managed to say a word. "Swine!" Then I leaped for the door, banged it behind me, crossed Dhuibert's room and found myself in the corridor—the staircase—the hall—the streets—the station—the train—in Paris.

People got out of my way after taking one look at me. On the platform a lady said to her little boy: "Look where you're going. He's blind." And yet I saw only too clearly. I saw Paule lying naked on the bed and Dhuibert standing over her with his clout—she lying down and he standing up, one in front of the other as in an obscene film. That image has lasted for more than eight years.

From the Invalides I went straight to my hotel in the rue Caumartin. No one paid any attention to me. I went up to my room, locked myself in, put the portfolio on my bed and opened the chest of drawers where I kept my souvenirs of Paule—her postcards, her little notes from Paris, her snapshots and the pink enclosure ticket from the famous Sunday in Vichy. I burned all of them over the wash basin without so much as a glance at them. This took a quarter of an hour (I put my watch on my bedside table for no particular reason), from ten minutes past eleven to twenty-five minutes past. I turned on both taps to clean up the mess. Then I went to the rue d'Astorg. I felt that everything I did was taking place outside myself. I thought of nothing, wanted nothing: I could only see Paule and Dhuibert, that was all. I was like a block of walking ice.

At the rue d'Astorg I, who always used my latch-key, rang the bell. Ernest, the office boy, opened the door. "*Mon Dieu, monsieur,*" he said. "Whatever has happened to you?" and I replied, "Nothing, Ernest, nothing at all." I did not recognize my own voice; in fact I did not even know I had spoken. I went to Maudière's door and pushed it open without knocking. The second time in one day I had entered a room without knocking! But this one was empty. Ernest, who could not help following me, told me that the Chairman would not be arriving until the afternoon, so I asked him to let me know at once when he arrived.

I went into my office and sat down and waited. I fixed my eyes on the little electric clock on the wall, but I continued to see that hideous image of Paule and Dhuibert. At five minutes past twelve the door of the typist's office opened behind me. I said, without turning round, "I'm not in to anyone." The door was closed.

Three hours passed. Ernest came in at exactly three o'clock. He could not say a word; he was so stupefied at seeing me sitting there with my hat on my head, my coat with the collar still turned up and the portfolio still on my knees—astonished, too, that I had not gone out to lunch. I understood that Maudière had arrived.

I went into his room, again without knocking. He raised his head in surprise. "Oh, it's you?" he exclaimed, and added, "Have you become a sleep-walker?" I laid my portfolio down in front of him and said: "Take it. I've stolen them." It was a black leather case with a little lock. Maudière, who continued to look at me out of the corner of his eye as though waiting for me to explain some joke, said, "I can't open it." I handed him the key.

He pulled out the bundles of notes one after the other. His face became more and more astonished. "How much is here?" he asked. "A hundred thousand—a hundred and fifty thousand?" "Four hundred," I replied. Then he grew angry. "Explain yourself, Gallon," he cried. I told him. Told him that I had forged a certificate and a receipt, that I had borrowed those four hundred thousand francs from a certain M. Perret de la Barre on M. Eskenazi's shares. It did not take me long to tell him that.

Maudière listened to me open-mouthed, the bundles of banknotes spread out before him. There was a moment's silence. Then he said suddenly: "Take off your hat, and turn your collar down. You look like . . ." I obeyed. "Sit down," he said, "or you'll fall." "No," I replied, but I sat down all the same. He asked me why I had acted like this and I said that I had no idea. He asked me if it was because of a woman and my marriage plans, but I replied, "What marriage?" He began to ply me with questions, and then I did not answer at all. He stood up and began to walk up and down the room, saying that he could not understand it. I told him that I could not either, that I had wanted the money, but once it was in my brief-case I no longer wanted it.

The discussion lasted an eternity. He spoke almost without a stop, and I hardly at all, always repeating the same thing. Then suddenly he went back to his desk and sat down. "Listen, Gallon," he said. "Obviously you've had a moment of aberration. I cannot possibly look upon you as . . . I must take your restitution into consideration. We will return this money to this M. de la Barre and you will give me your word of honour——" These words fell from me like water off a duck's back. I interrupted him, "There is another two hundred and fifty thousand francs that I cannot replace." I thought that Maudière was going to fall off his chair. "What?" he shouted. I explained myself as I had done about the second advance—no more, no less. "And where's that money?" he asked. "I've spent it." "How do you mean?" I did not reply.

I still saw Paule and Dhuibert, both naked. I had a headache and thought: He shouldn't ask me so many questions. He flew into a terrible rage at the idea that his signature should appear on Lévêque's certificate and that his company should have been so deeply compromised. He, who was usually so correct, began to swear. Then he said: "I am going to telephone to our board. You will spend the night in prison."

He took up the receiver and asked the telephonist: "Get

me Maître Dubosc." "He'll be in Court at this time," I said automatically. "Be silent," Maudière cried, but recalled the operator to get Dubosc at the Law Courts.

Well, Denis, to cut matters short, within the next two hours Dubosc lodged a complaint against me on behalf of A.P., Ltd., as plaintiffs; two detectives came to the rue d'Astorg with a warrant and they drove me in a taxi to my hotel to fetch a change of linen. They took the opportunity of telling the manager and of sealing up my room. You should have seen their faces. They all said, "He must have gone mad." Not a single word was exchanged between myself and the detectives throughout the whole journey.

At nightfall we arrived at the Law Courts. The magistrate submitted me to an interrogation as to my identity, and asked me a few questions—enough to learn as much as M. Maudière knew. Then came the Black Maria, all the formalities of being committed to jail, the noise, the slanging with a number of other offenders, and at last my cell—Division 8, No. 12 on the ground floor. That was that.

(*During the Night.*)

I AM lying down on my bed again staring at the ceiling, thinking of nothing and at the same time very unhappy. I can't explain why. I feel suddenly that I shall not be able to last the course if I continue to do nothing. The night is long. And then how can I know that it will be all over tomorrow morning? He is due to return at the beginning of the week, and Monday is only the first day. I am going to start writing to you again. I could not wait without you. But perhaps the reason why everything now appears to be so hard is because I have confessed everything to you.

A short while ago, as I drank my coffee, thinking of what I was going to tell you, I thought that perhaps the hateful image might vanish once I had got it off my chest. That does not mean that I shall spare him, but people say that confessions take a weight off your mind. A myth!

How would things have turned out if I had had a friend whom I could have turned to immediately before seeing Maudière? If, if . . . One does not bother about ifs when one is finished with existence. All the same, Denis, if he grants me a little more time . . . as I have already told you my story . . . As there is this pad of sky-blue paper, it is obvious that I should go on writing. I still have a mass of things to tell you and explain to you. Seven years, which demand it, and want their turn—not because of the jail. Do you know what prison's like, Denis? It's nothing at all, or rather—forgive me—it's something for people who still believe in life. Then there are not a great many solutions: they kill themselves, like Mornas or Corgoloin (they managed to hang themselves with nothing, for you become very ingenious in a cell), or else they revert to crime. Those are the ones that always return, and they are the least evil, the very ones who say to themselves: They won't catch me again. I won't commit any more stupidities. Unfortunately they have only to be faced with their old debts, their taxes and local banishment. Actually Corgoloin hanged himself during his second stretch, whereas I—I was already dead. And so the cemetery, prison, hell . . . But one day Death said, 'He must die too.' An idea. I should be incapable of recalling the moment it was born, and then it grew and took on strength with maturity—a fine child, one to be proud of.

Sometimes at Melun—because, of course, we were not allowed to speak ("I'll stop the first one that talks," cries the warder)—but people spoke all day; not me, the others—sometimes I heard someone mutter, "When I get out of here I'll get him!" I never thought of him like that, and yet I am going to get him all the same; but I am going to do myself in as well, and that is the difference. They want to avenge themselves to live in peace—for they imagine they can—whereas in my case it is to be at peace in death.

When I said that I did not know the moment when the idea first came to me, I meant that I did not think of it for some years. During the investigation I lived like a machine. I saw nothing but the image. I imagine it is for that reason that one or two of the newspapers treated me as a poor lunatic. They even wrote that the mystery of André Gallon did not exist. They were wrong. A magistrate would not have committed that mistake, nor would the doctor who examined me. Nor would Maître Fournier, although he saw me for only an hour. For Maître Fournier came to visit me (perhaps they told you). Please thank both of them for me, both him and his son, my school comrade Fournier! I did not know how to. I probably offended him. He came to the Santé on the second day. I had spent a sleepless night thinking of Paule and Dhuibert. From time to time I said to myself: Last night in your bedroom you dreamed that you held your fiancée in your arms. Now you are in prison, while she . . . But above all I saw Dhuibert.

In the morning they came to see whether I knew how to clean my cell—lift back the bed, scrub the floor and clean the slop bucket, just as in the days of Mother Mourgues, except that my cell was far more decent than that hovel of hers. The soup came at half past nine, but I ate nothing. I sat down on my chair. Suddenly, during the afternoon, I heard the key turn in the lock. It's a pretty sound, Denis, to hear a key being turned in the Santé, enough to make you expire if you are sensitive. The warder ordered me to follow him to the visiting-room. He led me between the cells to the top of a staircase and shouted, "Eight-twelve coming down!" Everything echoed fantastically in the silence—the lock, the steps and the voices. After a year on remand you grow accustomed to it, but the first time you find it very funny even if you are thinking of something else. I went down the staircase. A second warder echoed, "Eight-twelve!" and led me into a cell with a table and three chairs, where a very elegant gentleman in a cape was sitting at the table.

The door was closed and double-locked behind me. The gentleman said at once, "You used to be a pupil at Janson, I believe?" I hesitated a minute, for I thought, They want to get things out of me. Nevertheless I said that I had been. At this he offered me his hand and introduced himself. "I am Maître Fournier, the father of your school comrade." I said to myself, thinking of Fournier and you and everything, Ah, so they're coming round now when it's too late.

Maître Fournier told me that they had read about me in the morning papers, and he drew from his pocket a copy of the *Petit Parisien* (three colums with headlines)—"650,000 Francs Swindle. Secretary of A.P., Ltd., Embezzles" and beneath it "Returns 400,000 Francs. Is he Mad?" with a photograph of myself and one of Maudière. Maître Fournier told me that his son was very upset, for he recognized me from the photo and had recalled memories of the *lycée*, and asked his father to assist me if I had not yet chosen anyone for my defense. He had at once asked permission to see me. It appears that this was not at all regular, but the magistrate was anxious to please him.

I hardly thanked him. I still felt just as frozen and obsessed as the night before. I said that everyone knew the reputation of Maître Fournier; a member of the Law Council and a shining light of the Bar, and that I was not rich enough to choose a lawyer like him. I do not know what tone of voice I used but he looked at me curiously and replied (I remember his words): "You poor fellow! I'm not defending you in a professional sense. Don't talk about money, and tell me your story."

I gave him exactly the same details as I had given Maudière and the examining magistrate. He looked annoyed and told me that he could read all that in the newspapers and that he was asking for something else, my confidence. He assured me that in his defence he would never use an argument that would displease me or which I forbade him to use, but he *must* know everything. "If you don't confide in your lawyer," he added, "in whom will you confide?" I replied involuntarily, "In no one," and as I pronounced those words I felt to what an extent they were true, and that no one would ever know the truth.

Maître Fournier grew insistent and said that if I imposed such conditions he could not defend me, and that he regretted my obstinacy. He gave me to understand that normally one did not turn down a lawyer of his standing, particularly as I was in a precarious position. I replied, "So much the worse." He shook my hand, rang for the warder to open the door and added, "I shall ask the President to appoint someone good for you." He left and I remained alone with *them.*

On the way back to my cell I wondered why I refused to confide in anybody. Then I understood that I was ashamed, terribly ashamed. I had committed these terrible crimes for an innocent being, for the purest of pure young girls. For whom? For a whore. For I did not believe a word of Dhuibert's last conversation—the niece, the ward, etc. Never! If only he hadn't shown her to me naked. But like that, in her bed, she was no longer the same: there was nothing left of the Paule of my dreams. This was the true one. How could I have been near her for six and a half months in such incredible blindness? Can love deceive to such a point? No, it could not have deceived anyone else except me—because I was the Gallon boy, a poor fellow, a wretched fellow who had known the world only through porters' lodges and cheap furnished hotel rooms. No one else would have admitted such a thing. Can you see it? Paule X—I don't even know her name—Paule X convened by the magistrate and the judge roaring with laughter and saying, "That—your fiancée?" I would rather have had my tongue cut out.

But there was no need for this: I remained silent. And there you have the mystery of André Gallon and the 'incredible silence'. I became notorious because I was taken for a strong man, a first-class crook like Dhuibert, and I was treated accordingly. No Magistrate's Court for me, but the Assizes, and an investigation which lasted fourteen months. I was arrested on 13th February, 1928, and the trial took place on 5th and 6th April, 1929. Fuveau, the magistrate, could not make up his mind to let me go. At the beginning he made me appear every four or five days at least. Then he lengthened my 'visits' but he still saw me every three weeks or every month, and each time he repeated, "Are you going to tell me your secret today?"

I do not think that they comb the past existence of all criminals as they did mine. Those gentlemen would soon grow old. They knew everything, the least details—my prizes at Janson, my mother's places, Old Mother Mourgues—they even discovered comrades from the regiment whom I had never seen since. Maître Gaillard, my lawyer, was no less determined than Fuveau. He was a little younger than I was, an intelligent youth of twenty-four or -five and appeared even younger when he did not wrinkle his forehead. Council for the Defence! He was very proud of this title.

He remained with me hours and hours asking the most bloodcurdling questions. He even made a kind of investigation on his own account. He saw my mother, went to my hotel in the rue Caumartin and the previous one in the rue de l'Isly, to the Palois'. He said, "I will save you in spite of yourself." Save me from what? At the moment of the verdict, when the Judge sentenced me to eight years' penal servitude, he was furious with me. Up to the last minute he had hoped that I would speak; but when he saw he was wrong, I'm sure he began to hate me. He murmured, "It's absolutely your own fault that they've given you a stretch like that." I saw his hatred in the way he asked the question, "Of course you have not the slightest intention of appealing? Throughout the whole fourteen months he had said *us* . . . us! We shall plead this or insist upon that. Now it had become *you.*

He really had nothing to complain about. With his theme of the mysterious unknown woman and the honour of love being stronger than social conscience probably made me completely odious to the jury, but it had no importance—and so much the better for him if he was able to make a fine speech.

It's extraordinary to think how they must have studied me for fourteen months, tortured me with questions beginning with my banking account, which naturally afforded no surprises (except my loan to Dhuibert, do you remember, to pay his hotel bill at the Rembrandt, seven thousand francs, a bearer cheque, but as I paid it in again four days later this entry passed unquestioned)—yes, it's extraordinary that after so much research nothing came out about either Paule or Dhuibert. I admit that each day I, who never ceased to see them in my mind, though that I should hear their names mentioned—by the magistrate, by Maître Gaillard, by the head of the Santé himself who visited me three times in my cell. What most surprised this gentleman with the narrow head was to learn that I bought nothing from the canteen and was content with the infamous ration doled out to the poorest down-and-out. I, the man of the six hundred and fifty thousand francs swindle.

For example, why didn't they find Fernand the porter in the rue Caumartin who took Paule's two telephone calls on the day of their return to Paris and who shortly afterwards had been dismissed from the hotel? And Vichy? They learned through Maudière that I had spent my last holidays there and had stayed at the Imperator. Well, and what about my relations with the other guests? Nothing. Not the slightest allusion. I remained in ignorance until the trial. Then everything became clear when I saw Chinchard among the witnesses—Chinchard, called by the plaintiffs, by Maudière, as a witness to my morality. Actually he confined himself to saying that I went every morning to the casino and each Sunday to the races, but he could not say whether I gambled because he never left his office. The Judge asked him who my acquaintances were.

I was terribly afraid. These are the actual words of Chinchard's reply: "In town, I have no idea. In the hotel a casual greeting to one or two people but no particular friends." Ah, so that's it, I said to myself. Nobody mentioned the Rembrandt, not even he . . . The Rembrandt, the Imperator, the casino, were all forgotten for me. Paule naked, with Dhuibert naked before her, with the courtroom for background. No room for anything else.

I arrived at the trial in a complete stupor. Fourteen months of inaction in a cell. My fault in any case. I could have read, for there is a library in the Santé; or I could have worked—I could have made coal sacks if I had wanted to as they do in the Eighth Division—but I did not want to. Once I had cleaned out my cell I waited. Not even that: I endured. We had the right to half an hour's walk every morning, in little quadrangles whose walls I could see from my window, which were like the cages of wild animals with a boundary stone for a seat. Two of you were stuck in one of them and told to walk about. With a warder watching you from above? No, thank you. When they forgot to take me out I also forgot to ask. In any case they soon ceased to bother about me. Every evening at the beginning my grille opened and the prison orderly came and asked me if I wanted anything from the canteen. After I had refused for two or three weeks he gave it up.

It's quite simple: apart from the moment when my lawyer sent for me in the visitors' room, and the small visits in fine prison vans with the magistrate, I remained sitting on my chair, my elbows on the little table by the wall, and saw Paule and Dhuibert. When you think that we had supper at half past three and that the lights were put out at eight o'clock it certainly gave you a long time to do nothing. I should have let my beard grow if the regulations had allowed it, but it appears that this is forbidden for identification purposes. So I shaved twice a week in the corridor outside my door. I often hoped that the convict barber would cut my throat. One day I made a false movement but only succeeded in sacrificing a little bit of my right ear, and both of us were soundly rebuked.

While I was at Melun I never thought once, no not once, of those fourteen months at the Santé, and yet now that I'm writing to you my head is full of it. For example, I remember another day. I had just come back from the investigation where I had been confronted with Lévêque. (The poor fellow. He kept repeating: "Such a clean bit of business. All my liquid assets gone.") And as I climbed a staircase and turned into my corridor I saw painted on the wall:

Division 8
Nos. 2–14
Nos. 1–13

with an arrow, just like at the Imperator or the Rembrandt. But here I was not going to visit anyone: I was not left unguarded.

Sometimes I looked out of my window. As I was lodged in the top of the building I could see out over the quadrangles—a long building, a chimney, a dome and to the left the two prison walls with the tops of the trees on the Boulevard Arago. It was all sombre and sinister. Far away to the right there were other trees—chestnuts. I saw them burst into leaf and flower, turn russet and grow bare, and blossom again in the spring, but it brought me no more pleasure than the rest. You probably know more about the trial than I do if you were present or read the newspapers, for during the investigation and when I was brought before Fuveau of Maître Gaillard I followed everything that was said to me quite easily and when I did not answer I had my own reasons, but at the trial I could not concentrate.

The moment the guard let me into that hot, crowded courtroom—Paule and Dhuibert were still there, still there—I nearly fainted. I slumped down like a sack, and Gaillard said to me, "Don't look as if you are hiding yourself!" I wasn't hiding. How can you hide yourself when you are the accused and you are surrounded with people who have come to see you?

And on another occasion—the Judge had just questioned me about my childhood and about my father's glorious death—Gaillard said to me: "Don't answer like that, for heaven's sake. You'll give them the wrong impression." ('Them' referred to the members of the Jury sitting opposite me.) Deceive them? Had they brought me into this hall for me to bother about them? To deceive or to please them? If it amused them to judge a corpse . . . Of course, my silence exasperated everybody. The Judge barked that I was making a mockery of justice and the public murmured. I began to think: They will send me to Devil's Island, and then I shall see the sea. I also thought: What a pity I can't kill somebody—the guard on my right or the Judge or the prosecuting counsel. I should be condemed to death and it would all be over.

Nevertheless as the witnesses filed into the box one after another I went through some very extraordinary emotions. The whole of my past life . . . Madame Vinet, Provost, Alice, Palois from the rue d l'Isly, and Bloch-Templier who treated me as a Machiavelli, Jean Raphaël-Ambert, and Delaunay the head of 'Portfolio', Roussel from 'Financial Intelligence', Maudière and Chinchard, Lévêque and M. Perret de la Barre. But where was Maman? I said to myself: Where is she? (But I knew she had refused to come. They had read out her statement, which was by no means a tender one.) And *them?*

They had disturbed so many people. I can't think why. I hardly listened at all, but I watched: and behind the figures of Dhuibert and Paule I could see my life pass by. At moments I caught snatches, snatches of their testimonies. For instance, Provost said that I was reserved, almost sly. I have already spoken of Alice. Very few stuck up for me, and besides, how could they have done? Only Mme Vinet and Jean Raphaël-Ambert . . . She was convinced that I had been led astray, and the latter maintained that I should not be condemned until the mystery had been solved in spite of my silence. The prosecutor replied to this and there was a dispute in which Maître Gaillard took part. Maître Dubosc, who represented jointly A.P., Ltd., and M. Eskenazi rebuked Raphaël-Ambert, reminding him that he was one of the directors of the Bloch-Templier bank and as such should remember the wrong I had done to the establishment. There was an unbelievably stormy passage. Other witnesses provoked very sharp reprimands from both counsels.

In addition to my trial there was a second one to be held in the Civil Court between Lévêque on one side and A.P., Ltd., and M. Eskenazi on the other, for although the receipt which Lévêque held was a forged one the certificate was perfectly authentic. I admitted everything they asked of me but this did not satisfy Lévêque: he claimed his two hundred and sixty-five thousand francs and, in addition to that, damages. A.P., Ltd., on the other hand, contested the value I had quoted for the shares: the Company pleaded for reimbursement at their nominal value. The Judge tried to restore order by repeated assurances that this civil action would be decided in another Court. As for me, during the whole proceedings I saw Paule and Dhuibert. I was forgotten.

With the exception of the prosecutor. When the cross-examination began in the middle of the second day I wondered why this man hated me so much. His violence was ten times worse than Bloch-Templier's or Maudière's. Is it possible for a man to have his knife into another simply out of professional zeal? I had never been in a Court of Law before, so I had no means of comparison. But I cannot believe that this state official could whip himself up into such a state of anger to order. He would wear himself out in his prime. I listened to him with interest, and he noticed it. He stopped his tirade and pointed his forefinger at me. "Look at him, Gentlemen of the Jury. He knows how to listen when he wants to, our absentminded poet, our victim. Look at him on the alert." I could not help smiling at him.

In his opinion the case was simple. No accomplice, no evil influence and no being led astray: The day off I had requested from M. Maudière and the allusion to a marriage, pure Machiavellianism. I was a typical lonely egoist, and my whole life proved this. I quarrelled with my mother and was incapable of keeping a single friend (Provost). I had no mistress and spent no money. This was a proof that I had been waiting. Everything, according to him, pointed to premeditation. He referred to his white hair, his red robe and his thirty years of experience. He quoted cases similar to mine, and denounced my infantile tactics of silence as a clumsy ruse which astonished him in a man like myself. He threw a final pathetic appeal at me. "If I am not mistaken there is still time. Explain yourself. I strongly advise you to explain yourself!" Naturally I never breathed a word. "You have heard him, gentlemen. That is his answer." He spoke of the strong-box which I had obviously hired in a false name with false papers (we mustn't forget that this is the usual practice of forgers) in a bank in Lausanne or in Brussels, where the two hundred and fifty thousand francs of this poor dupe Lévêque would be waiting patiently for me until I had finished my sentence, etc., etc.

I have a good memory, haven't I, Denis? But this was also funny. Had the image of Paule and Dhuibert not been there I should have clapped him. As for my counsel, Maître Gaillard, I hardly listened to him. Why should I? Sometimes a raising of his voice or a movement of his sleeve in front of my eyes brought me back to his speech, but I had never worried less about myself than at this moment when my fate was to be decided. When, after his plea, I was asked if I had anything to add I replied, "No." I wanted to shout, "Down!" like you do to dogs when they bark at you. Dogs . . . We all have our day.

It took them more than an hour to come to a decision. I waited in a little ante-room with my guards and Maître Gaillard came in for a moment. He looked at me and said, "I'm more nervous than you are." I am sure it was at that moment that he began to hate me. Then I was led back into the courtroom to learn that I had been found guilty and sentenced to eight years' penal servitude. Taking into account the time I had been on remand, and with their way of calculating, I had to serve six years, six months and fifteen days—until October 1935. Without my remission for good conduct I should still be inside.

(Monday Morning.)

I LAY down on my bed, and this time I went to sleep. I have no idea for how long. When I opened my eyes it was still dark and I was hungry. I ate the bread and butter which they had brought up to me last night with my coffee, and then I thought it was ridiculous not to rest more completely, for an exhausted man is no good at all. I undressed and got between the sheets and fell asleep again.

This is the beginning of a new week. My last. Perhaps even the last day. As I dressed just now I wondered if I should not shave so as to look as I used to. If I did he would recognize me the moment I opened my window. But then I should have to go out and buy a razor, and I want to leave my room as little as possible. It's enough trouble going downstairs for meals. And what would they say here if they saw this sudden transformation? They might start asking questions. Well, so much the worse if he does not know who has killed him. Something deep down in him will be certain to let him know.

I have hung my overcoat in the cupboard and put my pocket-book in the inner right-hand pocket. If I were to keep it on me it might get soiled during my little personal operation. It contains your five hundred francs and nearly all my savings, four thousand one hundred and seventy francs. First of all you must reimburse yourself and then I should be glad if you would pay the hotel bill and give a good tip to the chambermaid. Here at least I do not wish to leave behind the memory of a thief, although it's true I shall leave the memory of being a murderer. Never mind. I shall have the better of the bargain. You can do what you like with the rest. If my mother happens to be in difficulties . . . But don't take them to her yourself or she'll throw them in your face. Send them by money order without the name of the sender. I shall be far away at that moment, gone away without leaving an address. . . . Perhaps the hotel proprietor will recompense himself handsomely, or perhaps my overcoat will fit one of the inquisitive people who will come and see what a suicide looks like. Well . . .

How blue the sky is! The shutters are open and the children will surely come out into the garden. They must go inside because I do not want to have an accident. I might perhaps miss with my first shot. No, I shall not miss. Besides, I have a feeling that it is bound to be this morning.

Oh, this waiting! I shall still go on writing to you. I am fond of you, Denis. In any case I have other things to tell you—things that will encourage me and assure me that everything will go off all right. For instance, how I learned at Melun what had happened to Dhuibert. In this matter something stronger than luck took a hand in the game: it was a sign.

First of all I must explain to you that after some time I had been given a new job. At the beginning, like all those who know how to read and write a little, I had been attached to the printing shop as a compositor, for at Melun there's no question of making up your own mind whether you want to work or not. In the Santé you are still looked upon as a man except that you have no name, but they leave you your clothes and your hair: you are a free man and have leisure to do what you like. After the sentence that's all over. With your shaved head, brown drugget and goloshes you can't fool anyone. You are a real convict. And you have to work hard and in silence, and without looking as if you wanted to complain. At the double too, and off with your beret when the chief warder comes round; and stand to attention when the whistle blows, and step off smartly and stop at the third whistle; and reveille at the bell, and to the refectory and to the dormitory at the bell. "I don't stop you thinking what you like," my mother used to say, but there it was best not to show what you were thinking.

Obviously a prison is not a place which develops a great deal of initiative or confidence in your superiors; but apparently the inmates do not deserve anything else. It's possible. In any case, you must understand, everything was a matter of complete indifference to me. To carry my obsession here or there, doing this or that, what did it matter? At the outset I was considered a rebel because of my dossier and my first clash with the warden when I annoyed him. I think I mentioned the occasion—it was the question of my religion. They kept their eye on me for quite a time, but one day they were forced to give me my good conduct stripe and a stripe for good work. No one was more surprised than myself, for I had acted and worked purely mechanically.

At the end of twelve weeks, or fifteen by their reckoning, I got a respite and was detailed to keep the workshop accounts. I spent five and a half years there without punishment or incidents. And when I think with what ease punishments were meted out all round me and all those who disappeared—in two minutes one could notice empty places in the refectory—for a little cure in the cells, I must say that I, who never used the least effort, must have had an extremely well-regulated mechanism. I'm wrong. Once I was put on the carpet and lost my good conduct stripe and had to pay a fine of five francs because I had dared to ask the chief warder why we weren't taken for a walk on rainy days. I imagine that the warders were frightened of rheumatism, for we were taken out twice a day after meals. We walked in single file round a basin with goldfish and a fountain as at Versailles. The fountain worked only on great occasions.

It was the same programme on Sundays and feast days. Those days we spent in the workshops or in the afternoon in the classrooms, or at religious service. We did not work of course, and those who wanted to could take a book out of the library, but we were not allowed to go outside. We had to wait five years for a new chief warder for that to be changed. Then at last we were allowed to sit out in the quadrangle and breathe the fresh air.

Each car that stops makes my heart beat faster. Perhaps he will arrive by the quay as his garage opens on to the Loire. In that case I shall have to wait until he comes out. I am all ready this morning. To start with my door is locked, and if anyone knocks I shall say that I am washing and ask them to come back later. Secondly I have put my table a little on the slant so that I have clear access to the window. I have unbuttoned my jacket. In this way I have only to put down my pen and feel in my hip pocket. I shall get up and at the same time open the window with my left hand. From the moment I see him appear I shall need three or four seconds, not more. If he walks as he used to he will not even get to the railings.

Well, for five and a half years I worked on the printing

shop accounts. Towards the middle of my sentence, in view of my good conduct, there was some talk of releasing me on parole, of sending me somewhere under sponsorship. Was this because I had never altered my conduct? The question had never arisen. But towards the end of last year the new chief warder took me aside one day and told me that I should probably benefit by a remission of six months. I trembled with happiness, because for me this was real liberty, the means of setting out to look for him. Six months' remission: the 24th April therefore. In the meanwhile I was transferred to the library. A favoured post–only two of you in a large, peaceful room behind the classroom, which is empty except for one hour a day, no surveillance and no bullying. There are of course, as everywhere else, bars at the windows, but you would miss them if they were not there.

I found myself here with a man of about fifty called Toutry. He was no more talkative than myself and we passed the first fortnight without exchanging a word. He was an educated man with a degree, who had been a little too personal in his dealings with a bank at Orléans and had been given six years. However, he was a newcomer and had been in our jail for only a year and a half.

He distrusted me for the first few days. Although he was treated with favour by the administration–I never learned why–he must still have been afraid of something and at the outset took me for a nark. Machiavelli! But he soon changed his opinion and began to tell me some of his life story in Orléans. As Dhuibert had told me in the old days that he came from the Loiret, I asked Toutry if he happened to know him. Without seeming to attach too much importance to the question of course, for I was sure that it would only call for another lie. Nothing of the sort. One of Toutry's relations, a local wine merchant, was on very friendly terms at B——sur-Loire with a certain Perrignier family who owned some splendid vineyards and whose vintage he bought each year. As a matter of fact one of the Perrignier daughters, the youngest of them, had married M. Pascal Dhuibert at the beginning of 1929 and this relation had been present at the marriage.

What do you think of that? Dhuibert had reappeared in his native district in the summer of 1928 like a prodigal son. Do you notice the date—1928? The year of my arrest. 1929 was the year of my trial. He returned with the aura of a great industrialist and the reputation of a Don Juan. . . . But it seemed that he wanted to make an end to all that and marry. Make an end of that, eh? I thought about that later. Perhaps he too had an image constantly before his eyes. An image? I should think it was rather a question of mistrust. After all, perhaps he was not a specialist in crookery, or perhaps he is continuing his activities in another way. In any case he must have got rid of her and come to terms with his accomplices if he had any—Chinchard anyhow. And then a quick return home to obtain the cachet of a respectable man.

Toutry also said to me: "At my age, you know, one marries a widow or a divorcee. Well, would you believe it, that lucky dog, who's probably older than I am, seduced the prettiest girl in the neighbourhood and the one with the biggest dowry. She adored him and still does today." I listened to everything without blinking an eyelid.

I also learned that they had bought a pretty little house on the banks of the Loire and that they had two children, two boys. Toutry added, "I saw an invitation to the christening of the second one not eight days before I got nicked."

A pretty little house . . .

I stopped writing for a moment. But then . . . waiting becomes intolerable. I was right to buy this second pad. It's already disappearing fast. The stupid thing is that I have no envelope in which to enclose this enormous letter to you;

so I have simply written your name and address with the word 'confidential' on the first page. I have put it in the cupboard beneath my overcoat. I have written the same thing on this continuation. When he appears I shall only have to put it on top of the paper and it will be found here in the centre of the table. One must be very credulous to believe that the word 'confidential' on an open letter would ever be respected. You never know. A thief and a murderer . . . but I shall also be a dead man, and there are people who respect the dead.

Can you imagine how my heart beat as I listened to Toutry! For years the idea of killing Dhuibert had gradually assumed the same proportion in my mind as the image. Tell me, shall I die with this image in front of my eyes or will it disappear at the moment I kill him? Shall I have one instant at least of respite? It would be wonderful if everything died with him, that I could kill myself *for myself* and not in order to kill him a second time.

If it disappears, Denis, I shall say that my gesture has vindicated my life and that I shall not have been a completely unworthy individual. My gesture—"A gesture? You've never made a gesture in your life!" was the insult which he spat into my face. He was mistaken: I shall have made two. Or then, if I am to be credited with only one, mine has not yet been made. I am waiting for him so that I can accomplish that.

What was I saying? Yes, how wonderful it was to learn after two or three weeks that I was going to leave Melun six months earlier than I had expected, and that I was not going to lose any time looking for Dhuibert. For once at least my fate wanted to do me a service. Had I still felt a shadow of hesitation such a sequence of circumstances would immediately have suppressed it. But as I did not hesitate in the least I simply thought: My sufferings will soon be over.

(A little later.)

I WRITE and stop. I keep writing and stopping. Until when?

There is one thing that I did not think I should tell you, but as it comes to my pen so much the worse. During those years at Melun, faced with that image that has never left my brain, I decided to kill Dhuibert; but I thought also of Paule. Not straight away, of course, but after three or four years. They were inseparably bound together in the image. And yet when I thought of her . . .

Denis, you who know the human heart, perhaps you will be able to say if she did not love me a little all the same. I have never known. I have stayed awake at night in that hole which was my cell—a cell there resembles a coffin, where it is never completely dark and where at every hour and at each round of the warders an electric lamp is turned on to wake the corpse—yes, many nights, wondering what would have happened if she had told me everything. Oh, I don't mean that loathsome story he concocted in their room. No, I mean if she had told me the truth—that he had introduced her as his daughter to get money out of me; that she was only a light woman but no worse than any other. I might have loved her just as much, perhaps more. After all, it was she who had inspired in me the taste for her purity. If instead of refusing my kisses she had given herself to me . . . That is the question. Did she ever want to—at least for a day? Did she control herself because she had to obey him, because she was his instrument? And what would have happened if I had not surprised them? I have tried to imagine events right up to the marriage, which doubtless neither of them had ever really considered. On those nights the image changed. I no longer saw her naked but in a white dress.

And in spite of everything on other nights I thought that she could not have been wholly indifferent to me. Anyhow, I have never felt the slightest desire to look for her–I mean after their separation. Nothing can change things any more. However, the day when——

There was a loud laugh somewhere. In the street . . . or perhaps in the house. The door . . .

It is he!

DATE DUE
